Loving the Lawman

Kirkwood Lake Romances
Book 2

Ruth Logan
Herne

DEDICATION

To Mandy... for giving us Mary Ruth
and a few other things as well.
Love you!

CHAPTER ONE

CHECKING HIS WATCH FOR THE tenth time in an hour didn't make the minute hand move any faster. Deputy Sheriff Seth Campbell frowned as he started to relock the door of his Kirkwood, New York, rental property. Boxes surrounded him in the retail area, but the person in charge of those boxes—his new lessee—hadn't appeared as scheduled. And that meant—

"Seth Campbell?"

He turned, surprised, because the back door of the old-world-style building faced the street, which was where he'd been looking. The lakeside door, overlooking the quaint boardwalk lining the sandy north shore of Kirkwood Lake, hadn't entered his realm of possibilities as an entrance in January. An icy wind accompanied the woman through the door. She shut it quickly and turned.

Huge, dark eyes met his gaze. Waist-length black curls tumbled from beneath a jaunty cap. A muted knit scarf that screamed money was knotted around the neck of her short wool jacket. Blue jeans and leather boots said she knew how to dress for fun, but one look into the depths of those eyes and Seth knew she hadn't had a lot of fun lately.

"Gianna Costanza?" He stepped forward and offered his hand.

"Yes." She gripped his hand and smiled. "Nice to meet

you after all our virtual back-and-forth. I tried calling—"
she held up a cell phone "—but it appears reception
in these mountains is about as spotty as mine was back
home in the Adirondacks."

"Technology is an amazing thing when it works," he
agreed. He swept a hand around the shop interior. "Does
it meet with your approval in person?"

Her quick smile said the character and warmth of the
vintage space pleased her, and that pleased him. "I should
pretend it's not up to par and see if I can whittle you
down on rent, but that would be outright dishonest,
because if anything, it's better than the pictures showed."

"Not too rustic or old-world?"

"Is there such a thing?" She shook her head, and when
she did, the tumble of hair shifted right, then left, untamed
by spray, which made him wonder if it could possibly be
as soft as it looked. She laughed at his expression, which
said there *might* be such a thing as too "old-fashioned,"
and walked to the nearest wall. "No, this is perfect. The
wainscoting. The chair-rail ledge for knickknacks and
artifacts."

"Dust-catchers," he noted, grinning. "My mother's a
big fan of them, too. Can't reason it out myself. Just more
to clean."

"Must be a woman thing." She smiled up at him, then
motioned to the right. "And the apartment is through
here?"

"Yes." He led her through a curtained door and showed
her around the unpretentious apartment. "I had time to
upgrade the shopping space, but the living area hasn't
received any intensive attention from my hands or bank
account yet."

"It looks fine," she told him. "Simple and clean-cut.
The furnishings are great. Having them here makes my
life a whole lot easier right now. Starting a new business
in a new town is work enough. Hauling tons of furniture

five hours cross-state didn't make my short list." She set a small, dark floral bag on the countertop. "The pictures showed a first-floor bedroom and a bath, right?"

"Right here." He took her into a well-lit room off the living area, and her smile rewarded him when she spotted the lake view. "You like this."

"My grandmother will love it," she told him. She pointed east. "I have her enjoying coffee at Tina Marie's Café. It was a long ride down and I'm afraid I tired her out." She stepped to the left, opened a door with an unadorned left hand and made a little face. "The bathroom is great, but may I ask one more thing of you?"

As pretty as you are? Ask away, sweetheart.

Reason reined in his teasing reply. He invited her question with a simple raised brow instead. Her smile lit her face in anticipation, brightening those dark, round eyes, and making the gold tone of her skin shine. But hitting on her probably wouldn't be the smartest move in the book because this was a business arrangement. Doing anything to make it go foul in a small, tight town would be stupid beyond belief, so he shoved the temptation to flirt aside.

"Could we install a bar in the shower? Is that too much work? Grandma gets around great, but I'm afraid she might slip if she doesn't have something to hold on to."

"Not a problem," Seth assured her. "My father owns the hardware store on Main Street. I can get a support bar in place by Monday."

"That would be wonderful, Seth." She moved back toward the living space. "Can we see the upstairs?"

"Sure." He let her precede him up the stairs, and her squeal of delight when she spotted the second floor made him smile. She turned in time to see the grin and made a face again.

"I'm sorry, I sound like a schoolgirl when I do that. It's utterly ridiculous. But this is so pretty."

Seth considered the two small bedrooms and the open lofted area overlooking the lake on one side and the living room and kitchen below. "It's loud."

She frowned.

"When there are people below, it's loud up here," he explained. "Terrible for sleeping."

"Ah." An understanding look said she was starting to get the picture. "You used to live here."

"Before I bought my house, yes. It was a great investment. My grandmother's family owned this building, so I bought it and fixed it up when I was fresh out of college."

"And your buddies would come to stay."

He nodded, then grinned, following her drift. "You're thinking that Grandma might not be as loud and intrusive as a couple of Campbell boys and their partying friends."

"Exactly. I don't think Grandma's knitting will keep me up, but thanks for the warning."

He laughed, and Gianna's heart went soft on the spot. A big laugh, hearty and full. The kind of laugh that saw lots of practice. She'd known that kind of laugh once. The sound of it called to her now, but she wasn't here for romance....

Not by a long shot.

Although Gram thought it was time for her to move on with her life and had spent over five hours of driving time reminding her that when God closes a door, He always opens a window.

Gianna knew that, hence the complete change in her life. Decisions she'd made before her mother and aunt left to spend the cold, long months of an upstate winter in Florida. By the time they came back north...

She shoved that thought aside and smiled up at Seth. "I'll have the moving van pull around to the apartment door and unload my things. You have keys for me?"

"Right here." He reached into his pocket and pulled out two sets. "I keep a master set for myself, so if you ever lock yourself out, I'm just across the street on Overlook Drive." He pointed through the window. "The white house with the porch on the double lot."

"A perfect family home." She smiled at the view and could just imagine a crew of kids racing around the wide, sloped front yard playing tag. Climbing the trees that were to the left.

Seth's smile disappeared. His shoulders looked suddenly heavy, and she had the oddest urge to wrap her arms around the big guy and give him a hug. But with her behavior labeled "strange if not crazy" these past few years, she curbed the impulse. Life had a way of messing people over. She knew that. Lived it. But right here, right now, was the new beginning she'd grabbed hold of a few months back. Months of praying, planning and implementation would come to fruition in Kirkwood, New York, overlooking the lake of the same name. Here she would embrace the life taken from her. The peace and hope of a new day dawning. She'd have the winter to settle in, and by the time the busy season rolled around after an early-April Easter, she'd be facing a new reality.

Would her mother understand? Would she embrace and forgive, or rage on in a mix of Italian and English and then cook pasta for the multitudes of Bianchis?

Time would tell.

Gianna followed Seth down the open stairs. He turned at the door. "Do you have help to unload?"

"I do." She pointed to the road, where a yellow moving van had pulled up. "My cousin and brother are my current minions. I promised them food to help me. They're Italian men so it really doesn't take much more than that."

"That works well on us Scottish guys, too," Seth admitted with a grin. She absolutely, positively refused to label his smile *endearing* or *sweet*. A smile was just a smile. Right?

One look up at him told her how wrong she was. Time to change the direction of her gaze. She turned and swung open the door to the small side porch. "The fact that I'm taking Gram off their hands sweetened the deal. Italian women are bossy by nature—something that doesn't appear to wane with age."

Seth laughed, understanding, while Gianna looked around the quiet, snow-filled, lakeside town. "She's going to love it here. I could see that the minute we rolled into town. For Grandma, this is like coming home."

Seth nodded agreement. "My grandma loved living in Kirkwood. It was her place, her town. Her history, she called it. Will your grandmother miss your old place?"

Gianna shook her head. "Not if there's a sewing machine handy. I get my affection for old things from her. She taught me to sew when I was barely old enough to thread a needle, and I loved it. So this venture into my own brick-and-mortar business is a big step for both of us, but I'm pretty sure she'll be content. I know I will."

"Well, good." He shoved his hands into his pockets as two dark-haired young men headed their way. "You guys need help?"

The taller one eyed the freshly shoveled driveway and shook his head. "I think we can back her up right here and unload to this porch. That way we can keep the snow and wet out of the house."

"I agree." The shorter man stuck out a hand to Seth. "I'm Mauro, Gianna's cousin."

Seth shook Mauro's hand and turned toward the taller man. "That makes you the brother."

"Joe Bianchi. Nice to meet you. You're the landlord?"

"Seth Campbell. I live over there." Seth indicated his house with a general wave across the street. "If there's anything your sister or grandmother need, I'm nearby."

"Good to hear since her entire family and support network will be over five hours away, in good driving conditions. With the exception of my seventy-something grandmother." Joe's tone scolded, but Gianna knew he meant well. Protecting her had become the order of the day after she had lost Michael.

You didn't lose him. He was taken from you. Stolen, in the dark of night. One simple moment of time, a twist of fate, and your life turned upside down.

It had, but she was determined to get her life back, with or without Bianchi approval. And about time, too. "Joe, really?" Gianna motioned to the truck. "Gram can outwork all of us, so it's great to have her on board with this new venture. Back the truck in here and let's get this done. We are not having this conversation again."

"That's because you don't have to deal with the multitudes of relatives on both sides," he called over his shoulder as he and Mauro headed back to the street. "But I'll run interference for you. It's what brothers do."

Seth turned, arched a brow, and the look on his face said she'd just become more interesting. "You ran away from home, Gianna?"

She laughed and shrugged as she stepped back inside. "In a manner of speaking. My family is American by birth but old-world Italian by nature. They like their ducklings to stay close to the nest, marry other Italians and raise a bunch of cute, Italian babies within five minutes of the family home. I'm bucking the trend." She let her smile include the old-fashioned setting surrounding them. "But they'll all be okay with it once I'm here and settled. The idea that I'm making a move like this while they're in Florida is giving my mother and aunt agita."

"Heart palpitations."

She tipped her face up to him as he moved to the door. "You're not Italian."

"No, but I've got buddies who've caused their mothers a little agita now and again. I get it."

She nodded as she held the door open. "They know we're moving here, but I didn't exactly do this with a nod of approval, if you know what I mean. By the time they come back north, Gram and I will be settled in. We'll be sewing up a storm of vintage-looking clothing for retail and special orders, we'll have the gently used clothing part of the store set up for business and all will be well with the world."

"Spring is a wonderful thing around here." Seth jutted his chin across the lamp-lit village road as he stepped outside. "Remember—I'm right over there if you need anything."

"I won't forget," she promised. She watched him walk up the slick black asphalt and thought how solid and safe he looked. Square-shouldered, light-eyed, brown hair cut short, flat on top, a don't-mess-with-me set to his jaw, his gaze. But when he smiled or laughed, his joy welcomed like a big, old hug.

And it was nice to know he lived close by. She'd mentioned that her mother was protective, but that was like calling a Category 4 hurricane a minor storm. She'd stretched the truth by minimizing her family's love and care. She had to, because she'd taken other steps without her family's knowledge, choosing a path that couldn't be backtracked.

If Sofia Bianchi—her mother—knew what she'd done, she might think Gianna had totally lost it. And Mike's mother, her former mother-in-law? Another battle to wage, even more difficult in some ways, but not yet. She'd bought time by moving this far away. Faith and time were what she needed right now. She had until spring to get things in order. Four months to make things happen before the older generation returned. And with Gram's help, that was just what she intended to do.

The subzero wind-chill seemed less irksome as Seth strode toward the café in search of an early supper. The diner would have their every-Saturday-meat loaf special, but he wasn't in the mood for meat loaf.

Tori hated meat loaf. Remember how often you pushed her to try it? Why did you do that? Was it really all that important?

Seth shoved the internal scolding aside to make room for the greater ache in his heart. Another Christmas gone. Another empty holiday put behind him. In the cold, late-day light of early January, darkness seeped into him.

What was she doing now? Was her mother cherishing her? Or was the girl's presence cramping her mother's style? And then what would Jasmine do?

Regret threatened to overtake him, but what would he change? Falling in love with the wild beauty of Jasmine on her good days? Or the grace and peace he found in the short years he'd had to father Jasmine's daughter from a prior relationship? Tori. Sweet, earnest, yearning for love, happy with the smallest things, not an ounce of greed in her.

You'd change the abandonment, his inner voice scolded. *And over two years of wondering where Tori is. What she's doing. And if Jasmine is taking care of her or putting herself first in typical style.*

He had no way of knowing, and despite being a cop, no way of finding out. So he hoped…and prayed…and tried to leave it in God's hands. But on quiet afternoons like this one, when there wasn't enough work to grip his hands much less his heart? On those days his mind leaped to various scenarios of where Jasmine was now and who was caring for her beautiful nearly twelve-year-old daughter.

Not one of the imagined scenes involved a picket fence and regular meals.

He sighed, hauled open the door to the café, forced a smile and hailed the owner. "Tina, how about a cup of coffee and one of your ham and swiss paninis?"

"With banana peppers, mustard and extra cheese." She slid the mug across the counter to him, made a little face of understanding, then reached out and patted his cheek. "Seth, you old bear, you don't wear your heart on your sleeve. It's plastered across that gorgeous Campbell face of yours for all the world to see."

"Long day."

"I see that." Her look of commiseration said she understood, but she couldn't. No one could.

If you spend every long, cold, snowy day feeling sorry for yourself, this is going to be one wretched winter. Get a grip.

Seth hauled in a breath and couldn't disagree with the mental reminder. His mother had framed a solid, plain-font version of the Serenity Prayer and hung it in his kitchen. On dark days like today, its simplicity helped. He still needed to learn to accept what couldn't be changed, but he was trying harder, and that helped.

He turned to sit at one of Tina's bistro-style tables and came face-to-face with a miniature woman wearing a black-and-white tweed coat. A bright red scarf lay draped around her neck. Coal-black eyes under a head of short, thick, straight dark hair said this had to be Gianna's grandmother. Her bright smile confirmed it.

"Company! Just what I wanted!" She pulled out the chair opposite Seth and sat down with the authority of seven decades. "I'm pretty sure I'd be in the way over there—" she hooked a blunt thumb over her left shoulder indicating the western end of Main Street "—so they tucked me here, but winter afternoons in a lakeshore community aren't exactly teeming with business."

"Can't argue that." Tina smiled at the woman, refilled her coffee cup and set Seth's sandwich down in front of him. "Seth, this is Carmen Bianchi. She's moving into—"

"My place on the water." He reached across the table to shake her hand, and the strength of her grip didn't surprise him. Her knowledgeable look said she was letting the younger generation think they'd taken control. For the moment, she'd let them live under that illusion.

He liked her straight away. "Are you hungry, Mrs. Bianchi?" Seth indicated his sandwich and the bowl of fries that followed. "There's plenty here. Or we can order you something."

"I just finished a piece of Tina Marie's ham and broccoli quiche, and it was excellent," she explained, with a glance at the schoolhouse-style clock on the side wall. "I've already decided I'm going to annoy her by being a regular customer until she gives up the recipe."

Tina grinned from behind the counter. "We love regular customers. Annoy away."

"Somehow I don't think you're ever an annoyance, Mrs. Bianchi." Seth handed over the basket of fries, smiled when she helped herself, and added, "Unless you're bossing folks around who think they're running the show."

"I like a man who reads things well. You're a cop, right?"

"A sheriff's deputy," Seth replied. "How'd you know?"

"You sat facing the door. You're carrying a weapon in your back right waistband. Your eyes say gentle but your chin says you'll do what needs to be done. My husband was a state trooper for thirty years."

"You're not too shabby at reading people yourself, Mrs. Bianchi."

"Call me Carmen," she told him, and helped herself to another fry. "And Tina Marie, you should come over here and chat with us until it gets busy."

"Add matchmaker to her list of attributes," Tina joked

from where she was washing stoneware in the small, double sink. "I learned a long time ago to steer clear of the Campbell boys, though, so thanks anyway. Heartbreakers, every one."

Seth pseudo-whispered after swallowing a bite of his sandwich, "That means she's still pining for my brother who's stationed in Fort Bragg."

"As if." Tina frowned at him, then winked at Carmen. "Max had his chance. What normal woman would find a big, rugged Special Forces operative appealing?"

Carmen laughed out loud. "What woman wouldn't? I love young people." She leaned forward, still smiling. "I'm so glad Gianna and I have moved here. Our little mountain town is lovely, but so lonely in winter. And winter wears out its welcome long before the thermometer brings us a reprieve."

Seth knew the truth of that, but the café door opened before he could reply, and when Gianna Costanza breezed in with a gust of fresh, cold air, his need to talk disappeared.

The softly lit café brightened in her presence. Snowflakes dotted her shoulders, her cap and the spill of curls falling down her back.

"Gram! I'm so sorry. I didn't think it would take this long to get all our stuff moved inside. But you've found friends, I see." She flashed her smile to Seth and Tina Marie as she arched a brow. "And if that's a panini right there, I'd love one to go."

"Or you could take a breath and eat right here," Carmen said.

"I'd do that except that Mauro and Joey need to be on their way," Gianna answered. She turned more fully toward Tina. "Actually, can you make it three paninis? With fries like the big guy has?" She smiled at Seth, then extended her hand across the counter to Tina. "I'm

Gianna Costanza. Gram and I are opening the vintage
clothing store in Seth's rental space on Main."

"Wonderful."Tina gripped her hand with an answering
smile. "This town needs more women in charge."

"Or just more women in general." Seth stood, grinned,
then tweaked Tina's short brown hair as the other ladies
laughed. Tina gave his arm a friendly whack before
turning her attention to Gianna's order. He turned back
toward Gianna and Carmen."If you ladies need anything,
I'm just across the road."

"Thank you, Seth." Carmen's smile said she appreciated
his offer.

"Actually, there is something else I meant to ask you
about." Gianna moved a step closer."I need to install rack
holders on the exterior walls to display the used clothing.
And hooks above to showcase styles or finish a 'look.'
Can you give me the names of carpenters I might be
able to hire?"

"Sure. Give me your phone."

She looked puzzled, but handed over the phone. It
took Seth mere seconds to pull up his name. Under the
"notes" section he put *carpenter and renovator*. He handed
the phone back and waited to assess Gianna's reaction.

He might crash and burn.

Or win the day…

She burst out laughing, and Seth notched a mental *x*
into the "win" column.

"Do you actually have time to do this?" she asked.
"And are you really a carpenter?"

Carmen inhaled sharply.

The older woman's dark expression surprised Seth.
"I'm a deputy sheriff by day and a guy who loves to work
with wood on my days off. With Dad in the hardware
business, do-it-yourself became a required phrase for
Campbell kids to learn in pre-school. But mostly, I love
that old building and would rather do the work myself,"

he explained. "Draw me a sketch of what you're thinking, and I'll get the supplies this week. I've got next weekend off, so if I gather what I need in the next few days, I can probably have the job done by mid-month, in plenty of time for your opening."

His words dimmed her expression, as if he'd lowered a shade over a lamp-lit window. Regret tightened her pretty features. "I'd hate to put you out. Let me call around and see if there's anyone who can jump right on this for me. With your approval as property owner, of course."

Seth went straight from the "win" column to "crashed and burned" in the space of a few seconds. That made Carmen's expression more note-worthy, but Seth could read the writing on the wall. He had no intention of crashing or burning ever again. Not on purpose. The last time took his heart and nipped his soul.

Keeping his face relaxed, he shrugged one shoulder toward her new shop. "Just let me know who you get so I can confer with them. That old building was built strong, but I'm partial to it, so TLC is important to me."

"Will do." She offered him a quick smile and moved to the counter, waiting for her to-go order.

He'd been dismissed. So be it.

He turned to say a quick goodbye to Carmen, but the look on the Italian woman's face as she gazed at her granddaughter, a look of anguish mixed with love—

Seth's heart melted. He was a peacemaker, by birth and profession. He championed the underdog, helped the oppressed, carried a gun and wore a badge because it fit his nature. Carmen's look of concern said these women had a story.

So did he.

And if they respected his right to privacy, he'd do the same, because life was better when compassion ruled the day. But he still wanted to know who would be working on his grandmother's building because family legacies were important.

People matter. Buildings can be rebuilt.

While that was true, Seth shrugged off the internal warning. He knew how to control a piece of wood and a hammer. Years of being Charlie Campbell's son meant the entire clan understood at least the elementary skills of building and refurbishing.

Women?

He'd been put through the wringer in the past and had no intention of risking a similar fate anytime soon.

CHAPTER TWO

"I'M NOT SAYING YOU SHOULD marry the guy." Carmen dipped her chin and sent Gianna an exasperated look over her reading glasses. "But you haven't found anyone to do the wall braces, and you'll end up running out of time for a pre-Easter opening."

"Then we'll open for May instead," Gianna retorted.

Carmen lifted a silent, knowing brow.

Gianna huffed, tossed her work onto the table and picked up her phone. When she got Seth's voice mail, she left a terse message and hung up, then went to make tea, an annoying replacement because what she wanted was a tall, hot mug of coffee, but coffee didn't make the list of desirable beverages for the moment.

She missed coffee, but the rich scent of a robust blend turned her stomach, so tea had become the drink of the hour, a sorry replacement for an espresso lover. That thought darkened her already feisty mood.

Four separate remodelers had been unable to do the job she needed done. Calling Seth after dismissing his offer? That rankled. While the town of Kirkwood was small, she'd thought someone in the little city of Clearwater might have been looking for a quick job, but no. Her job wasn't big enough for anyone to make repeated drives to the north tip of the long, tapering lake midwinter, and none of the more local renovators were available.

Which made her grandmother correct again and pushed her to call her landlord after rudely dismissing him the week before.

The apartment's doorbell rang while the tea steeped. She spotted Seth's profile and wished her heart didn't jump.

But it did.

She reached for the doorknob with damp palms.

Ridiculous.

And when he turned and met her gaze as she swung the storm door his way, a tiny sigh got trapped somewhere between her heart and lungs. She choked it back, motioned him in, then noted the tape measure he hauled out of his jacket pocket. "You came prepared."

He didn't smile like he had last week.

Why would he? You cut him down like sharp scissors to cotton. Quick and precise.

Because she had to. She knew that. But knowing didn't make it any easier, not now, in his presence. A waft of something deliciously spicy came her way as she followed him into the shop.

"Carmen, how are you?" He gave her grandmother a long-lost-friend greeting, and Gram had the nerve to pop up from her chair and hug him.

"Good! I love this place, Seth, it is *perfetto* for our shop, for the work Gianna and I do. Even the snow I do not mind. Its beauty is of nature and God, and everything is so close to walk to. And the view." She clapped a theatrical hand to her heart, and Gianna couldn't help but smile. Her grandmother was never afraid to let emotion rule the day. "I could look upon this beautiful lake forever."

Gianna had learned the hard way to shield her emotions. How many family and friends had advised her to grab hold of her life and move on? To go back to New York City and immerse herself in the hectic lifestyle she'd embraced for years before she'd met Michael and fallen in love?

She'd kept hold of her life. What she lost was her husband, gunned down on his day off. The irony of that bit deep. A New York State trooper on a convenience store run for his pregnant wife, stumbling onto a robbery in progress.

Gone, just like that, and then the miscarriage a few weeks later.

Emptiness had consumed her. Some said for too long, but what did they know? Had they suffered her loss?

No. So they could—

"Do you have a sketch?"

She stuffed the backward trail of thoughts aside and picked up a sheet of paper from the counter. "Right here."

"Thanks." Seth didn't say any more. He simply took the sketch, crossed to the east-facing wall, then measured repeatedly between the red cedar beams.

"I was thinking four-foot sections here, here and here." Gianna pointed out the separated wall areas for him. "If we leave every third or fourth area free, I can strategically place mannequins to display complete outfits."

"Those headless things give me the willies," he muttered as he penciled numbers. "Although the ones with heads aren't much better."

"Dress forms," Gianna told him.

He paused and frowned. "I don't get it."

"Like that." She pointed out the dress form in her sewing corner. "I'm working on a circa-1940's gown for a customer, and the form is adjustable. When I'm sewing, I use the form to see if I'm nipping and tucking in all the right spots as I create the dress. Out here—" she waved a hand to the stack of boxes and rolling racks clogging the middle of the room "—I can display things in their natural size so that customers have the advantage. What looks great on a size six doesn't always work for a size sixteen."

"You're making this?" Seth stepped closer to the form. He touched the soft, tucked fabric of the sleeve and turned her way. "I thought it was some old-fashioned gown you bought. This is lovely."

The way he said it, as if he understood the tiny differences between good- and fine-quality garments, made her feel better inside. "Thank you."

"This isn't sewing," he went on as he admired two other outfits on the rack behind Gianna's sewing corner.

She arched a brow and looked up, waiting for him to finish.

Time stopped. So did her heart, and if the look on his face was any indication, his reaction mimicked hers, so she took a deep breath and a full step back. "It's not?"

"It's art. Like a fine painting or a book you can't put down."

He needed to stop talking. He needed to stop being so nice, so kind, so capable, so big, strong and handsome. If you weren't working in the garment district or with a costume designer on Broadway, sewing skills were relegated to the occasional alterations shop these days. Her grandmother's skillset was becoming a lost art, just like Seth said. But not on Gianna's watch. She may have given up the streets of the Big Apple, but she wouldn't abandon the God-given artistry of their combined efforts. Their location on the quaint and upscale lakeshore would provide a tremendous tourist trade, while special orders on the internet helped balance the books.

She retreated one more step, but it wasn't far enough, because the spiced wood scent of him called to her. She'd answered that call once, to a man who wore a uniform, a man with a badge. She'd loved him, heart and soul.

She'd lost him the same way.

He'd work when Gianna was out of the shop, Seth decided as he left his father's hardware store later that afternoon. Charlie Campbell had called in an order to an Illinois supplier. Seth knew what he wanted for the dress bars. He wanted stressed metal, old-looking, but strong. Racks of clothing were heavy. The walls in the house were solidly made. The racks into solid support beams. The rustic tone he selected complemented the antiquated building, the classic decor he'd labored over when Jasmine had divorced him. Working in the cold, long days of that first winter had been his personal therapy, just him, some tools and a propane heater for long, silent days.

He'd been foolish, he saw that now. He'd charged forward into that marriage regardless of his mother's misgivings, and Jenny Campbell never discouraged casually. Despite that, he wouldn't regret the time he'd had with Jasmine's daughter, Tori. Like Garth Brooks nailed in that beautiful tune, if he hadn't opened himself up for the pain, he might have never gotten the opportunity to be Tori's dad, to be a father. His heart ached, wondering where she was. What she was doing. And because Jasmine had never allowed him to adopt the girl, he had no legal right to know.

That reality hit hard.

He contemplated grabbing takeout from the diner, but a glance at his watch refuted that thought. He and trooper Zach Harrison were assigned to oversee security and traffic flow for the year-long bicentennial celebration the town had kicked off in late October. Using both departments, they would coordinate security efforts to cover back-to-back lakeshore activities, and tonight's planning meeting was important. He put his stomach on hold, grabbed two coffees at the café and headed to the town hall. Zach's SUV was parked to the right of the building. Seth walked in, saw Zach, strode forward and handed him a fresh cup of coffee, then turned when he heard a familiar laugh.

Gianna and Carmen sat side by side in the third row, center aisle. The wind-driven snow hadn't kept attendance down tonight. Even with the crowded conditions, the two newcomers stood out like tropical birds in a sparrow's tree. Nothing about the Italian women said low-key, and speculative brows and whispers crossed the full room. The two seamstresses seemed oblivious, heads bent over a legal-sized pad of paper on Gianna's lap, her pencil moving in swift, bold strokes.

"Zach, Seth, you're both here, good." Tess Okrepcki made a note on the pad in front of her before she faced the room full of volunteers and vendors. "And because Zach is on duty tonight, I suggest that we move the security portion of our meeting to the first item on the agenda so he can get back to work. Any objections?" Nods of assent said the people agreed. "Then a show of hands, all in favor?"

Hands shot up all over the room and Seth's stomach did a happy dance of celebration. If he and Zach could get out of the meeting quickly, he'd find food that much sooner. And a nice big burger might take his mind off the pretty woman seated in the middle of the room. For ten minutes, anyway. Until he saw her lights blink on across the street from his home in the middle of the night. Either they were both nocturnal, or she didn't sleep any better at night than he did. And that made him wonder why she'd have trouble sleeping.

He turned as Tess rambled something about historically correct attire, determined not to think about Gianna Costanza. His resolve lasted about six seconds.

"And I'm thrilled to announce we have two new expert seamstresses in town. Carmen Bianchi and

Gianna Costanza have offered their services to help make costumes for our bicentennial volunteers. Carmen is a long-established seamstress from Hamilton County in the Adirondack region of New York State, and her granddaughter Gianna worked on Broadway as a costume maker for six years before moving back to her hometown in the mountains. Gianna and Carmen, would you stand up so everyone can see you?"

See them?

The two well-dressed women had been the topic of room-wide speculation for the past ten minutes, but Tess pretended oblivion.

Carmen and Gianna stood, smiled and waved to the crowd, then sat back down amid a smattering of applause.

"Law enforcement, can you give us your report?"

Seth stepped forward as Gianna turned. Her eyes went wide, seeing him. Her mouth opened slightly, as if his presence affected her. One hand clenched the other. The gesture said he made her nervous.

Welcome to the club. He smiled at Carmen, gave Gianna a polite nod, then delivered his report in quick, crisp terms.

"Wonderful!" Tess scanned the committee members before she moved on. "Questions, anyone?"

"Will the mounted patrol be available for any of our summer activities?" one woman wondered. "They always add a special element to our gatherings."

"They're scheduled to help with the Fourth of July festival and the Labor Day waterside celebration," Seth explained. "But they're patrolling the park and forest preserve the rest of the summer, and we have to be careful not to short our fellow officers during their busiest time of the year."

"We're grateful to have them here in Kirkwood for those two events," declared Tess. "Zach, Seth, thank you so much for your attention to detail, and please extend our thanks to your departments. We've got approval from your captains to allow you out-of-uniform status for several bicentennial functions, so if you could both make appointments with either Carmen or Gianna, they've agreed to create historically correct uniforms for you."

"Say what?" Seth stared at Tess, then switched his gaze. Gianna looked just as surprised as he did.

Carmen didn't look surprised at all. She stood, waved to Tess and didn't seem to care about meeting protocol, another reason to love the aged woman. "I'll set up a time with our officers so they can be on their way. You go right ahead with the meeting," she advised Tess, as if the committee chair needed permission. "Gianna can offer advice while I'm gone."

She stepped into the hallway, whipped out a smartphone and flipped to her calendar app with greater speed than Seth had ever been able to muster, then arched a look to Zach. "Would you prefer to come to the shop together?"

"Less scary that way," Zach muttered. "Do we really have to do this, ma'am?"

"Carmen," she told him firmly. "And yes, I guess you do. If the captains say do it, the officer does it. At least that's how my late husband saw it, and he had the promotions to prove he knew how to handle the work and politics of policing a community."

"Can't argue that," Zach replied. "Together's fine. Then we can complain in unison."

"I'll have *pizzelles* and Italian cookies for you," Carmen promised. "If the mouth is full, complaints become a non-issue."

Zach laughed. "I like how you think. Okay, how's this Saturday? Does that work for you, Seth?"

"I'll be there working on installing the rack hardware, so yes. But I thought you were planning to be gone on Saturday?" He met Carmen's gaze straight on. "I distinctly remember you saying that you and your granddaughter were attending an all-day function in Clearwater."

"When the opportunity to help the town came up, we decided this was more important," Carmen replied. "Helping with the bicentennial costuming gives us the chance to show off our versatility without spending advertising dollars, and you know how pricey that is for start-up businesses."

Her reply made perfect sense, but Seth wasn't a wet-behind-the-ears beginner on the force. He saw the old woman's ruse and couldn't fault how she wrapped her matchmaking in a shroud of community outreach. Clever and admirable. And he'd make sure to never underestimate her in the future, which was good since they were neighbors.

"Ten o'clock okay?"

"Fine with me." Carmen tapped a number into the calendar as the next person filed out of the room to set up a fitting time. "Officers, we'll see you Saturday morning." She turned and aimed her bright-eyed smile at the next victim as Zach and Seth left the building.

"Did we just get railroaded into wearing some kind of Dudley Do-Right costume to become laughingstocks of the entire community and thousands of tourists?"

"Yes." Seth sighed, stared out at the snow, then shoved open the door. "Worse, my Saturday just morphed from a peaceful long day of me, hardware and pre–Super Bowl radio sports chatter to me, them and Italian opera."

"No way." Zach's look of horror matched Seth's spoken angst. "Bring your phone and earbuds. Stream a service."

"No earbuds."

"Borrow some," Zach advised as he moved to his car. "I get to leave and go home, where our current topic of conversation will be what color to use on the nursery."

"Piper's expecting?" Seth clapped the other man on the back. "That's wonderful news."

"It's early, and we're not saying much yet, but yes, come

summer we should have a little Harrison to add to the bicentennial fun."

"Congratulations." Seth meant the word sincerely. "There's nothing like being a dad."

Zach met his gaze. Seth read sympathy mixed with Zach's joy. "Thanks, Seth."

Seth climbed into his car.

He'd been starving when he showed up at the meeting. He wasn't a bit hungry now. He was thrilled for Zach and Piper. Their fall wedding had been a fun, hometown event. And Seth's younger brother, Luke, was engaged to Piper's sister, Rainey. Their wedding would join two families who'd met life's challenges and clung to faith and hope.

Right now all he could think of was his empty house. No schoolbooks strewn here and there. No inane, overacted tween shows on cable. And no one to urge to eat meat loaf…or try broccoli…or teach how to tie flies for stream fishing, or take out in Dad's boat, watching for nesting water birds. There was just him and eight yawning rooms, a house that felt so empty he could cry. But big, strong men didn't cry, so he parked the car, grabbed a shovel and spent two hours cleaning out his driveway and then Gianna's. By the time he completed the job he was tired enough to fall into bed and sleep.

And that was a scenario he'd been practicing for over two years. Work himself so hard that he couldn't help but sleep, and while he was awake, pray that God watched over the girl he loved as a daughter. Wherever she might be.

"Police officer uniforms?" Gianna scolded as she grabbed a snow brush from the trunk after the lengthy meeting. Two hours in lake-effect snowfall had left the car buried. "Really, Gram?"

"I can't think of a better way to show off tailoring skills than on those two," Carmen quipped back as she reached for the second brush. "Everyone will notice, guaranteed. Those men are seriously good-looking."

The thought of Seth in an old-style sheriff's uniform wasn't unappealing.

The idea of working with him was, but only because she could deny the attraction when he wasn't around. In person?

She sighed, swept the snow aside with more vigor than necessary and took out her aggravation on innocent frozen precipitation. By the time she climbed into the driver's seat, the car had begun to warm. She sent a sidelong look to her grandmother, who waved off her concerns with practiced nonchalance. "We're here to do a job. A new start. Doing what we do best and having people's gratitude and awareness is huge, Gianna. You know that."

"I get that part." Gianna thrust the car into gear and moved forward carefully, eyeing the thickening snow. "But I wasn't expecting police uniforms in the deal. Fitting uniforms is a pain in the neck."

"I found patterns online. They won't be any more trouble than the long, tucked skirts we're doing for the ladies."

Gianna disagreed silently. She'd have no problem working with the ladies. Nipping the waists, adding tucks for proper ease over the hips.

Working with Seth?

That was a problem in itself. Her fault, she knew, so she'd just have to deal with it. Right now she had other things to think about, though. Like how to get the car into the snow-clogged driveway so the overnight plows wouldn't hit her small SUV and send it into the nearby lake. She turned onto Main Street, put on her signal, then smiled.

He'd cleared the driveway. From side to side, and end to end, black asphalt with just a little clinging snow called to her. The crunch beneath the tires said he'd sprinkled salt, too.

Quick tears stung the backs of her eyes.

Mike had taken care of her like this. Always thinking ahead, thinking of others. That warmth and bravery led to his death. If trouble loomed, he jumped in, wanting to help. Serving and protecting, all of his days.

Maybe Seth wasn't like that. She hadn't known him long enough to know. But they shared the caregiver's urge, the guardian. Looking out for others.

Was she selfish to avoid a repeat of those qualities? To resent what was taken from her? Maybe.

But better selfish than heartbroken again.

As she stepped out onto the firm surface, she reached back to grab her purse and notebook.

Light streamed through Seth's side window, one single beam from within. Outside, his porch lights glowed all night, a policeman's first line of defense, she knew. Overnight lights made it tough if not impossible for anyone to creep up on a house. But somehow Seth's lights didn't look protective. They looked welcoming. Waiting. As if he turned them on to guide someone home, like that old George Strait song.

But that was silly female imaginings. She closed the car door and followed her grandmother inside, worried and excited about Saturday. And the fact that she was excited to work with Seth worried her even more.

CHAPTER THREE

"I'M NOT SURE WHERE WE are, Dad, I just wanted to call and say I love you." A tiny sound that could have been a choked sob broke through Tori's whispered phone message. "I miss you so much."

Seth's heart ground to a halt as he listened to her plaintive words again on Saturday morning.

Tori was reaching out to him. She'd done this before, but not in a while, and he'd hoped...no, he'd prayed... that the interim silence meant things were going better. The pain in her childlike voice said that wasn't the case.

The phone call had no return number. She'd blocked it so he couldn't call her back. That meant she'd be in big trouble if her mother knew she'd contacted him.

A harsh pain in his chest said his heart had started beating again. How could he help her? How could he reach her?

He'd exhausted legal means early on. Because of his nonparent status, he had no recourse. His fault. He should have insisted on the adoption first thing after they'd married. At least then he'd be her legal father. He'd have rights. As it was, he had nothing, and when Jasmine had left, she'd taken the most precious thing she'd brought to their ill-fated marriage. Her child.

"Seth, good morning." Reverend Smith stopped at

the road's edge, his half-grown pup straining at the leash. "Titus. Leave it."

The dog paused, sighed, then sat, obedient, but his expression said he wondered why they were stopping on the cold, wet street when there was a perfectly good rectory a block away.

"Titus is doing well." Seth leaned down and rubbed the pup's neck with gentle hands. "Zach's sister took one of the pups for her boys, and he's more rambunctious."

"Living with boys will do that." The reverend laughed. "I saw your face as I approached. I know that look. You're troubled about Tori, I'm guessing."

"She called me."

"Ah." Reverend Smith's gaze shadowed. "And did her phone call leave you a way to reach her or her mother?"

"No."

"And so your heart was just re-torn."

Seth stared beyond the minister's shoulder, to the flat edge of ice inching across the lake as winter's cold thickened. "Not like it ever really mended, Reverend."

"A wound reopened tends to fester."

"Yes."

"And winter is a long, cold, dark season sometimes. Not the best for healing."

Seth eyed the growing snowpack along the lake's edge and lifted one shoulder. "I don't mind it. And no, I'm not making excuses," he added when the reverend arched a brow. He breathed deep and swept his gaze across the lakeside village, quiet and still on a snow-filled weekend morning. "Winter's peaceful. I like the snow. And I love seeing storms come in, watching them recede. I've got a great vantage point up there." He pointed to his hillside home. "The hard part is that I can see the edge of the interstate as it cuts across the water below the 'point.' And when I see that, I think of Tori. There are days when I have to fight the urge to jump in the car and go after her.

Find her. Bring her home. I know I can't do that, but that stretch of road calls to me. And after hearing the sadness in her voice—" he tapped the belt pouch that held his phone "—I'm tempted more than ever."

The pastor reached out and clapped a hand on each of Seth's shoulders. "You have a good heart and a strong mind, and I can't believe God won't fix this somehow, someway. And that's what I'm praying for. That God mends this chasm to bring you peace of mind and a healed heart."

Seth accepted the blessing, but he couldn't wrap his head around such a thing. Peace of mind would only come if he could keep Tori safe. And a healed heart?

His heart was doing okay. It had healed enough to know he wouldn't chance getting it broken again. And that was a promise he could make.

"Good morning!" Gram's welcome meant the boys in blue had arrived. Gianna took a deep breath, put a pleasant and somewhat blank expression on her face and stepped into the sewing area at the back of the shop. She tried not to stare as Seth settled an armload of tools and boxed braces along the front wall.

"You'll still be able to do this today?" she asked. She pointed to the equipment he'd brought in. "I was afraid we messed you up with the fitting appointment."

"Lotta day left," he told her, then winked.

Her heart did a theatrical spin—most unprofessional. Her face refused to let the attraction show. "That's wonderful. If you'll—"

"Zach, come in, thank you for helping your friend. So nice!" Carmen bustled forward as if on cue, which made Gianna figure she'd been watching for Zach's entrance from the doorway leading to the apartment. "Set those down right here and I'll take you over by my area."

"And I'll send Seth right behind him," Gianna added. She sent her grandmother an I-know-what-you're-doing look as Seth organized the equipment into some kind of order.

"If we both measure, we get done in half the time." Carmen tossed a tape measure across the room.

Gianna caught it in one hand, met her grandmother's grin and decided to stay mum. There would be no arguing in front of the two policemen, but later?

Gram would get an earful.

"Where would you like me?" Seth faced her with the look of a man doomed, and despite her internal efforts, she had to smile.

"I promise it won't hurt. Much."

"The last time I heard that was when the doctor had to reset my broken arm. And just so you know? It did hurt. A lot."

"Aw." She made a face of sympathy up at him and touched his arm. "I'm actually sorry you had to go through that."

"I was, too. But we got the bad guy and he's doing time, so justice prevailed."

Her heart longed to protest his easy take on an uneasy topic. He'd gotten one bad guy and a broken arm. But there were bad guys everywhere. And not all the good guys walked away with just a cast. Some never walked away at all.

"What do we do first?" He tipped his gaze down to her and for just a moment she let herself get lost in those clear blue eyes. His hair was rumpled from wearing a hat, but the tight Scottish curl didn't allow hats to crush his hair, so she found herself looking up at a modern-day Celtic warrior with a great smile.

Focus. You've got a job to do. So does he. And that's it.

"All you have to do is stand there for a minute today."

"Can do."

She unwound her measuring tape as her grandmother chatted with Zach about his family and farming and all the innocent things Gianna could discuss if she was doing the state trooper's measurements.

But no, she was measuring the single sheriff's deputy with the great chin, and for the life of her, she couldn't find a thing to say that didn't seem flirtatious or mention his job. And she refused to do that. She reached up and measured from his neck to where his wrist met strong, broad hands.

Do not think about his hands. Their strength. That scar on the back of his left hand that looks fairly new. Eyes on the tape measure. Got it?

Oh, she got it, but it was impossible when she had to go eye to eye with him to measure his neck. The scent of fresh outdoors mingled with guy soap, a combination that made her long to draw closer for one more whiff....

So she stood back, jotted *17.5* in her notes and moved to measuring his chest. While doing so she decided that life was not fair, men shouldn't be so amazingly well built and she'd probably have to resort to bodily harm of her conniving grandmother for putting her in this situation. At least she was experienced enough to be able to discern his measurements without needing him to remove his shirt. Ten years ago, she wouldn't have known how to adjust for the slight difference.

Now she did, although seeing Seth in a T-shirt couldn't be considered punishment.

Waist...a trim thirty-two.

She finished her task in a matter-of-fact manner, jotted numbers into her sizing notepad, then closed the small notebook. *Done.*

"No hip measurement?" he wondered.

"Not for men." She shook her head as she looked up, and the gleam in his eye said he was kidding.

"Jerk."

He laughed and tugged a lock of her hair as he stepped back into his shoes. "Couldn't resist. I've been measured for monkey suits for way too many weddings. No one's ever gotten quite this nervous about it, though. Although you hid it well."

The fact that he recognized her nervousness meant she hadn't hidden it well. The blush she'd tried to control steamrolled her cheeks, but she made a concerted effort to keep this exchange strictly business. "Measure twice, cut once. I expect you employ a similar ethic when working with wood."

"I do. And just like good fabric, certain grains give me more trouble than others." He arched an innocent brow, but she was fairly sure he lumped her in the "certain grains" category. "We're done for now?"

"Yes. I will turn this—" she patted a bolt of tan cotton "—into this." She held up a pattern of an old-style sheriff's uniform and grinned when Seth looked reassured.

"That's actually kind of cool." He touched the fabric lightly, and there was no mistaking the relief in his tone. "I like that Andy Griffith look. I was afraid we'd have to wear some overblown thing with ugly brass buttons."

Gianna sent Zach a look of sympathy. "That would be his."

"Ha." Seth laughed and clapped Zach on the back. "You'll look like a band leader in a parade. Perfect."

"I'll still be carrying a gun," Zach warned, and Seth laughed again.

"I'm going to leave off some of the braid," Carmen told Zach. "The state police dropped the braid and the tails on the coat fairly early, so I'll do the same. I promise you will not be a laughingstock." She reached up and patted his cheek. "My husband gave decades to the troopers. I treat his counterparts with utmost love and respect."

"Thank you." Zach smiled down at her as he lifted his leather jacket from a hook behind her work area. "I'm going to head back home and help my wife and my father compute how many cows are *too* many."

Seth offered a quick retort as Zach moved toward the door. "Knowing your wife and father, I don't think there is such a thing."

"I can't disagree." Zach sent him a rueful look. "And with the new barn nearly complete, I see a busy season ahead of us. But truth be told, I couldn't be happier, so bring on the cows. Ladies." He turned and tipped his cap in their direction. "Thank you for making this relatively painless."

"You're welcome." Gianna smiled at him, then turned toward Seth. "Is it easier for you to work on the clothing racks if we're not here? If it is, Gram and I can make ourselves scarce. I know we said we'd be gone today, and sometimes it's a pain to have people underfoot while you work."

Would it be easier to work if she disappeared behind that long, rippled curtain?

Definitely.

Then he wouldn't have to pretend she wasn't there. Breathe her amazing perfume that was nothing like anything he'd ever smelled before. But they were neighbors. Moreover, he was her landlord, so he had to get used to working with her. Or at least working *near* her. And while he hadn't thought he was in the market for anything romantically inclined, when Gianna drew close, it wasn't close enough. And he was old enough and mature enough to know that meant his interest extended beyond a friendly handshake.

Hers didn't. *Correction:* She was tempted, but determined to remain off-limits, and he'd had enough of difficult women with Jasmine, so he was all right with maintaining distance. He respected lines drawn in the sand. So be it. He set up his saw at the north end of the building and flexed a shrug. "I can ignore you if you can ignore me."

Her eyes went wide, then narrowed, and Seth was pretty sure the thought of being ignored didn't sit well with the Italian princess at the opposite end of the room. He didn't like it all that much either, so he'd wait and see what she'd do. Eyeing the long expanse of walls, he had plenty of work to keep him busy. And at least they weren't playing that horrible, boring—

Orchestral strains broke into his train of thought, deep strings with a slow, haunting percussive backbeat. He could bang his head against the wall right now, or man up and pretend he didn't notice, but when some guy began belting out all the angst of the world in some foreign language, he reached for the earplugs he'd brought along and almost hugged the packaging. Some guys used ear plugs for the most minute sawing jobs. Not Seth, but Gianna and Carmen didn't know that.

Let them think he was protecting fragile ear drums. And he was, in a way. Because his eardrums would be okay if he never listened to opera again.

She'd redone the side seam twice, a ridiculous novice mistake because it was a simple seam, straight and thin.

Easy when there isn't a wonderful man working ten yards away, wearing well-washed Wranglers and a perfectly fitted dark knit turtleneck.

He was humming something, too, something that didn't meld with Pavarotti's majestic tenor, and as Gianna plied her seam ripper for the second time, inspiration hit.

Seth was wearing earplugs. For the drill's noise?

Or the opera?

Chagrined, she realized that just because *she* was a huge fan of the singing stage, a guy like Seth might want to tear his hair out rather than hear the deep operatic tones and strings repeatedly. She moved to the apartment, spotted her grandmother catching a midday catnap in the living room overlooking the snow-swept frozen water and turned off the music feed to the shop. When she came back through the curtained door, the only noise was his slightly off-key rendition of "Fields of Gold."

Seth liked Sting.

So did she.

She retook her seat in the well-lit sewing corner and hummed along with him. The new quiet bathed her in peace, the melding of her voice with his soft and unassuming. The duet was broken from time to time as he mounted the bars high enough to avoid street-length dresses grazing the floor. Just before he turned on the drill to set bracket holes in the next section, he turned, frowned, then smiled.

Oh, that smile.

Her heart melted. Her fingers stuttered and the business end of a pin bit the tip of her thumb. She jumped back, not wanting to taint the gauzy fabric with a prick of blood, and Seth moved to her side instantly. Concern erased the smile, and he grabbed for her hand. "Are you hurt?"

"No, just silly."

He looked puzzled momentarily, then awareness dawned. He snatched the earplugs from his ears and pocketed them. He examined her hand, seemed to decide she'd most likely live and dropped it back into her lap. "Sorry. You just looked scared there for a minute."

"Only because blood won't wash out of dry-clean-only fabric," she told him. She pressed a small pad of white cotton to the tip of her finger and nodded toward the far wall. "The brackets look good. I love that stressed bronze color."

"It fit."

"Yes."

He started to turn back to his work, then swung around again. "You turned off the music. You can listen if you want. This is your place now."

Add considerate and self-sacrificial to the list of attributes she liked about this man. She shrugged, checked her finger, then reapplied the pad to make sure she'd stanched the tiny cut. "Compromise is a good thing when people work together. You're not an opera fan, I take it."

His face said more than his reply. "No."

She laughed. "Well, did you know that Pavarotti and Sting have sung together?"

"I'm not sure I believe it, but I'll ask—when?"

"On *Pavarotti & Friends*," she explained. "The producers arranged for all kinds of musicians to perform with him. Rockers. Jazz. Classical. My father was highly insulted, but I loved it." She sent him a pointed look and added, "Pavarotti and Sting sang *'Panis Angelicus.'*"

"I love that hymn," Seth admitted. "It's majestic." He drew up a chair, pretended to check a nonexistent watch and said, "Break time. Is it a rule that if you're Italian that you must love opera?"

"It should be," she teased. "I love the rise and fall of voices, and I don't care if it's opera, a barbershop quartet or a strong choir. The synchronized timing of music and voice calls to me." Memories swept her. Made her smile. Broadway. The Met. Concerts in Central Park. "I worked in New York after college, and I had the opportunity to see all kinds of things, a multitude of cultures. An amazing experience."

"Will you go back?"

The question hung between them, suspended in midair, as if her answer meant a great deal, as if their casual conversation could lead to something stronger.

More permanent. But that was silly. "To visit," she told him. "My home is here now."

He smiled again, but it wasn't the amused smile of moments ago when he'd realized she'd switched the music off. This smile held the warmth of hope and the promise of spring. "Well." He stood, brushed his hands against the sides of his thighs and squared his shoulders. "The finger's okay?"

"Fine, thanks."

"Then I'll get back to work."

"Me, too."

Everyday words, simple and sweet. But as she watched him cross the room, his gait relaxed, she knew she hadn't shared easy conversation with an attractive man in a long time.

She'd dated occasionally after losing Michael. And she'd had fun from time to time, but she'd *worked* to have fun, putting forth concerted effort so her dates wouldn't think she was a total waste of time.

Enjoying moments with Seth required no work. That slow, comforting gaze. The big, blue eyes. The firm chin with the tiniest cleft when he smiled.

He didn't need her to impress him. She liked that. Too much, most likely, but since there was nothing to come of it, she'd enjoy the opportunity to have a new friend, as long as that was all it was.

Old-world beauty.

The phrase struck Seth when he pictured her, tucked in the corner behind him, the whir of the pricey sewing machine a soft hum beneath her hands. A cloud of delicate fabric covered her lap, and she'd clipped her hair back, away from her face. The combination of the curls and the puffs of gray fabric were a Renaissance painting come to life.

He kept his eyes on the wall and the drill, his gaze focused on the sturdy brackets needed to brace the movement and weight of hanging garments.

But his thoughts? Those were ten yards back, on the pretty girl sitting at the pale blue machine, the motorized pause and go of intricate work keeping her in his mind.

The scent of something amazingly delicious captured his attention midday, about the same time as a knock came at the street-side door. Gianna started to stand, but Seth waved her back down. "I'll get it. You keep working."

He didn't wait to see if she obeyed him, but when he opened the door, his mother stood on the snow-crusted sidewalk. "Mom."

"Hello." She breezed in, flashed him a smile, then held a basket high. "Gianna?"

"Yes." Gianna stood, settled the fabric onto the chair and rounded the sewing table. "I'm Gianna Costanza." She put out her hand in welcome. "You're Seth's mother."

"Jenny Campbell." Jenny handed off the basket and waved it toward the kitchen in the apartment beyond. "I wanted to welcome you and your grandmother to town. I'd have been here sooner but one of our grandsons was sick and I took over with him the past few days so his parents could work."

"Is he doing better?" Gianna asked, and it didn't surprise Seth to see genuine concern in her eyes. "I hope so."

"Much," Jenny told her. "He had fifth disease, nothing major, but I wanted to keep him away from Piper if possible because she's quietly expecting."

"Not so quiet if half the town knows," Seth scolded.

"This isn't half the town. It's you and Gianna. And Zach was in here earlier and I expect he said something."

"Nope."

"Oops."

His mother looked chagrined. Seth laughed and looped an arm around her shoulders. "We won't tell. Will we?"

He shifted his gaze to Gianna. She shook her head, but a hint of worry glazed her eyes. "You okay?"

"Fine. Yes."

Carmen bustled in from the apartment side of the building. "Hello! You're Seth's mother?"

Jenny introduced herself. Gianna handed Carmen the overflowing basket and watched as her grandmother led Jenny into the kitchen. But when she turned, worry creased her brow.

"Are you sure you're all right?"

"Tired, I think." She made a face at the chair. "Too much sitting work makes me sleepy. I think I'll take a quick walk."

"Sleepy equates walk?" Seth stepped closer. "Usually the way to conquer tiredness is to nap."

"Fresh air works, too." She grabbed a thick jacket from a hook around the corner and donned it quickly. "I'll be back soon."

She was out the door in a flash, and when Carmen poked her head through the connecting door, Seth just shrugged. "She went for a walk."

Carmen waved it off as if it wasn't outrageously rude behavior. "She can't sit too long working. She's an action-motivated girl."

"Who sews for a living." Seth hiked a brow in Carmen's direction. "Odd, right?"

"Not at all," Carmen answered smoothly. "Come on in here, I've got chicken soup, and your mother brought homemade bread. We'll have a quick lunch before we get back to work."

He shouldn't, even though Gianna had left. He'd promised himself he'd keep their relationship professional. Distanced. Being caught in the shop with Gianna so close showed him the unlikelihood of that. Just knowing she was there, sewing, humming now and again, made him feel at home.

He couldn't afford to feel at home here.

Why not? His conscience scoffed. *She's nice, funny, talented and creative. Did I mention drop-dead gorgeous?*

Seth got all that. What he didn't get was the vibe she emitted, keeping him at bay. He'd obey his instincts... *his other instincts*...and maintain degrees of separation, no matter how much his heart softened in her presence. Soft hearts led to one thing: soft heads. And he'd been in the fire too much of late. He had no desire to get burned again.

Fifth disease.

Gianna hurried across the road, turned left at the first of two traffic lights and climbed the steps to the library. Warmth greeted her.

She barely felt it.

Children laughed in a semicircle off to her right as the librarian held up a funny-looking puppet and squawked, "Hi! I'm Skippy Jon Jones!"

The children giggled as the librarian continued the story. The puppet interrupted regularly, his raucous voice teaching on a kid-friendly level. Their joy of learning without knowing they were learning flooded Gianna with anticipation, but the thought of this childhood disease concerned her.

She sat at one of the computer screens, clicked it on and waited until she could do an internet search, then sighed in relief when she saw that most people contracted the virus as youngsters and carried that immunity into adulthood. A simple blood test would tell her if she was susceptible to the disease or had already had it.

That meant she needed to find a doctor, and that was something she would do first thing Monday morning. She'd relocated her grandmother and herself by promising her family that she'd look after Grandma. None of them were aware that Grandma was currently the caretaker of the two.

They'd know soon enough. She shut down the computer, then grabbed a couple of books so she wouldn't look like an idiot when she walked back into the shop. She signed up for a new library card and headed back down the road, wondering if Seth would think she was totally whacked.

Some days she wondered herself.

"You're back!" Her grandmother's bright smile said everything would be fine. Just fine. "Jenny has brought us homemade bread, and I just put on water for tea. And I do believe there's a tray of chocolate walnut brownies in that pretty basket."

"My weakness. Well. One of them," Gianna admitted as she slung her jacket back onto the hook. She set two books down on the counter, trying to make it look like her trip to the library had been crucial.

"*Raised Bed Planting* and *Turn-of-the-Century Patterns, Volume 2.*" Seth surveyed the books once he stood up. He pulled out a chair for her, then carefully slid it in behind her as she sat. "No time like the present to ponder June's gardens, I guess."

His gaze skimmed the snow-filled front window.

He wasn't buying her library excuse for ducking out. He might not know why she'd left in a hurry, but he wasn't about to believe it was to grab two obscure books before the midafternoon library closing.

He probably thought she was darting away from him. And since that was exactly what she *should* be doing, she let it go. "This looks wonderful," she told Jenny as she reached for a thick slice of fresh bread. "And Grandma made herbed oil to dip it in? This is a treat."

Seth started toward the door.

Gianna turned, surprised. "You're going back to work already?"

He indicated the wall clock with a jut of his chin. "Play-off game today at four. I've got a date with my recliner."

"Of course." She smiled, and didn't think of how nice it would be to spend the late afternoon watching football with him while the current storm blustered outside. She wouldn't think about the coziness of a shared afghan, steaming hot coffee and a big bowl of chips.

She'd sew.

That was what she'd come here to do, after all. To build a business with her grandmother's help, to work toward summer with one eye on the clock and one foot on the sewing machine treadle. She had goals. Timelines. Objectives. Nothing could get in the way of that. But seeing Seth move into the shop area to continue his work made a part of her wish she'd been invited to watch the late-day game with him.

Would she have said yes?

Probably not, although she'd like to.

But she would have enjoyed knowing she'd been welcome.

CHAPTER FOUR

"OH!" "Easy now." Seth gripped Gianna's arm to keep her from falling, fairly certain that if she went down on the icy walk, he and Carmen would most likely follow. "Keep hold of Carmen, there."

"I've got her." Gianna huffed a breath up to get a stray lock of hair out of her face, one arm clutching her grandmother, the other held tight in Seth's grip. He used his free hand to tuck the errant curl back behind her ear, and if his hand lingered there a few seconds too long, well…

He smiled down at her because her expression said she got what he was doing and didn't mind it near as much as she made out, even if she meant to offer total resistance to his charm. "Better?"

He released her arm and indicated the hair by switching his gaze. "It seems to have a mind of its own."

"I should cut it," she grumbled as she tested the footing beneath them. "I had no idea this was black ice."

"Don't cut it, it's gorgeous. And this side of the street is notorious for black ice this time of year because the sun hits it just long enough in the late afternoon to melt things and leave the surface slick. Then it takes its own sweet time to melt the following morning."

"Seth, thank you." Carmen aimed a bright smile up at him. "We could have fallen."

"My pleasure." He fell into step beside them and touched his hand to Gianna's elbow a couple of times, ready to grab hold if she faltered again. She didn't, and that made it tough to figure out a reason to hold her in the short minutes before church services began. "Would you ladies like to sit with me?"

"We'd love it!" declared Carmen. Her decisive nature sounded a great deal like his late Grandmother Campbell. Tough, strong, caring, the kind of woman who did what was needed, whatever it took.

"But we can't." Gianna refused his offer with a slight frown at her grandmother.

"There's no harm in sitting with a neighbor to share the Lord." Carmen met Gianna's grimace with a wise smile that only made the younger woman's frown deepen. "Seth, do you sit on the right or the left generally?"

"The right, but I'm becoming a creature of habit too much of the time." He pointed to the church and then stepped back. "You pick. No one in their thirties should be this predictable already. It's wrong on multiple levels."

"Gianna said that exact thing before we moved here," Carmen agreed. "How about this? Right in the middle. And I did like Reverend Smith's sermon last week about allowing children to grow. Stretch. Reach."

"Taking chances worries parents," Gianna reminded her.

"Taking chances once you've hit thirty shouldn't worry anyone," Carmen retorted. "God gives us one life, one vessel. Our job is to live it well and take care of ourselves."

"I can't find fault with that," Seth told her. He allowed the ladies to enter the pew, and wasn't sure how Carmen maneuvered it, but he found himself sitting on the aisle next to Gianna, with Carmen tucked to her right.

Candlelight flickered across the front of the historic church. The Christmas decorations had been removed. Part of Seth liked the uncluttered look of the sanctuary and altar, but another part lamented one more holiday gone. A Christmas past.

A light tap on the shoulder pulled his attention. His parents slipped into the pew behind him, followed by his brother Luke, Luke's fiancé, Rainey, and three five-year-olds. His mother tempted Dorrie to her side with a book about Noah's Ark. Aiden snuggled himself between his father and his future stepmother, still looking a little peaked from the virus he'd had that week. Sonya spotted Seth and crept around the edge of the pew. "May I sit with you, Uncle Seth?"

Her endearing entreaty made his heart stretch open. So did his arms. She climbed onto his lap and slanted an uncertain smile toward Gianna and her grandmother. She blinked twice, slow and sweet, then snuggled into his chest as the music began.

Gianna smiled back at her. Carmen did likewise, her broader face crinkled in joy. The joy of a child, a gift from God. Holding Sonya made his heart ache more and his soul ache less, his very own personal enigma.

Seth lifted her as he stood, holding her close to his side, not caring that she was five years old and perfectly capable of standing and sitting as the service required. It felt right to hold her, to show her the correct passages and tilt the hymn book just so, as if she could read the words with him. She couldn't, but she liked pretending, and that was okay by Seth.

Joy and sorrow, seamed together. Gianna read Seth's expression as he held the little girl, and she wondered what created the mix of emotion. Would he tell her if she asked?

Maybe. Maybe not.

And yet, she longed to know. Longed to soothe, to comfort. And when a miniature quarrel broke out between the two little kids behind her, this little girl burrowed farther into Seth's shoulder.

Endearing.

Her head filled with what-ifs. Thoughts of boys and girls, babies and children, cradles and car seats vied for mental attention. And when a baby started crying at the back of the church during the kind reverend's sermon, the comforting sounds of the mother's murmur made her wonder if she truly had what it took to be a mother.

Her phone vibrated on the short walk home after the service. She pulled it out, recognized her former mother-in-law's number and was tempted to let it go to voice mail, but she couldn't. She stepped to where a parking lot met the freshly plowed sidewalk and said hello.

"Gianna, how are you? How is your grandmother? Is everything well, everything all right?" Marie Costanza spoke in rapid-fire sentences ninety percent of the time. The other ten percent was spent sleeping.

Gianna drew a breath and offered reassurance. "We're good, Marie. In fact, we've just finished church and we're heading home so it's not a good time to talk. The walkway is icy, and I need to hold on to Grandma. How is Fort Myers?"

"Cold! Wicked cold. I wonder what I'm thinking spending all this money to come down here and it's cold, no matter! What about there? Is it bad? Snow? Ice? Cold? Too cold?"

Gianna had learned that when Marie fired too many questions, the best line of defense was to attack the middle ground. "To be expected, right? It's winter, this is Western New York. One plus one equals cold around here. But I hope it warms up there for you. And you've got friends around, right?"

"Friends, yes, friends are good, but they are not the same as *famiglia*. Not the same as being around my brother, my sisters—although all they do is yak, yak, yak! And you, my Gianna. Whenever I think of my Michael, on those nights when I miss him so much I cry, I think of you and how happy you were together. That wedding, so beautiful. Never have I seen a happier bride, and why not?"

Her words claimed Gianna's heart because she'd been absolutely blissful back then. So much change, so much gone, a bend in the road she'd never expected. And now another.

"And you made Michael happy, you made his life good." Marie put heightened emphasis on the word *good*. "This is what a mother wants for her son, what we pray for, night and day. A woman who will stand beside him and love him all the days of her life, no matter what. I thank the good Lord that he had that with you, Gianna. If only…" Her voice trailed off.

Gianna understood "if only." If only she hadn't miscarried twice. If only Michael hadn't made a convenience store run to buy ice cream for his pregnant wife. If only he'd been home asleep, in bed, like most people were at eleven o'clock at night.

But no, he'd taken her request to heart and drove five miles to get her a quart of mint chocolate chip. Her favorite.

He'd lost his life trying to keep her happy, and it had taken a long time before the heavy guilt of that eased. And she hadn't eaten ice cream since. "I know."

"Ach, I should not speak of sadness, I know. I know. I just wanted to see how you are, how your grandmother is doing. You will open your store soon, I think?"

"Six weeks, give or take."

"So long? Why?"

"We're getting things set up in the shop and we've

gotten some special orders to do for a local celebration. But most of my vintage-look stock has arrived, we've got the wall-mounted display bars in place and I can start unpacking boxes and racks soon."

"I should come back. Help you."

Gianna's heart jumped into high gear. The last thing that could or should happen would be to have Marie here, now. "No, no, no. I won't hear of it. Grandma and I are doing just fine and there's only so much room, Marie. You'll be back before you know it. Then you can come visit. Enjoy your time in the sun. Once it shines again, that is. And we'll be here waiting to see you in the spring."

Please don't come, please listen to me, please don't—

"You're right, of course. I have Bella with me and I can't leave her here alone while I run back there."

"Of course not." Bella was Marie's aunt, a nice woman, but she'd never have gone to Florida alone. For Marie to leave meant Bella would leave, too. Or be desperately unhappy.

"I'll call, then."

Relief flooded Gianna. "Anytime, please."

Phone calls she could handle. Having Marie there, in person?

No.

She needed more time before facing that reality. Michael's mother wasn't a bad person, but life had soured her on some things and jaded her on others. When it came to family matters she was strong, assertive and somewhat aggressive. Losing her only son, the only child God had gifted her, had broken Marie's heart. Gianna understood that quite well. "Talk to you soon."

"Goodbye, Gianna. God bless you."

He had.

Gianna wanted to whisper those words. Better yet, she longed to scale snow-filled peaks and shout them from the tallest mountain. Maybe take out an ad in *USA*

TODAY and announce her blessings to the world, but not yet. Right now she needed to plan, focus and bide her time.

As they passed the family diner, a horrid scent accosted her, assailing her senses.

Her mouth began to water. Her throat constricted, and the rise of nausea quickened her steps. The plowed sidewalks had the familiar crunch of fresh salt to melt ice and aid traction, but even with that, Gianna wasn't sure she'd make it home before she got sick.

"Gianna?"

Seth's voice, coming from her right.

"Honey, are you all right?"

Carmen's tone, warm and solicitous, to her left.

She didn't dare open her mouth to speak, or turn either way. She hurried into the house, glad they'd left the door unlocked, and rushed to the downstairs bathroom.

Cooking meat hadn't sat well for weeks, but she'd been better recently. Today?

Not so much.

When she finally came out of the bathroom, Carmen sent her a mixed look of love and sympathy. "My precious girl, I am so sorry. Here." She took Gianna's arm and led her to the gray tweed couch. "You sit. Put your feet up. Rest for a while, okay?"

Gianna sent her a watery smile. "I'm okay, Gram. You know how it is."

"I remember well," Carmen agreed. "It is not something one forgets."

"They say it's a good sign."

"A well-set pregnancy makes its presence known," agreed her grandmother. "But *bellisima*, I would love for you to just be comfortable and then have this baby. That is my wish."

Gianna laughed. "Mine, too, but life just sent us a dose of reality, Gram. Can you get me some ginger ale please?"

"And crackers?"

"No." Gianna leaned back against the soft pillow, eyes closed. "Just the ginger ale. And tell me again how hungry I'm going to be in a few weeks because right about now? That sounds next to impossible."

Pale. Gray. Distressed.

Seeing Gianna like that made him want to help, but what could he do?

Frustrated, he'd watched Carmen follow Gianna into the house and he'd stood silent, at a loss. Should he offer help? Yes? No?

Common sense pushed him home. He needed to get out of his church clothes and make sure his things were ready for the night shift he'd taken to help his commanders out of an influenza-induced shortage of personnel. Then he'd come back across the street to finish the four shorter display bars strategically placed to feature complete looks, according to Gianna.

Whatever those were.

When he got back to the vintage store about forty-five minutes later, she looked better. She sent him a smile as he strode in, and his quick assessment said whatever was wrong had abated, and at this time of year, viruses swept through town in waves. Still, he couldn't resist crossing the room for a closer look, just to make sure.

Those eyes, so brown. They had a deep, rich tone with no pale lights, so dark they overwhelmed the pupils within. Pale gold skin, the kind that tanned like crazy, without a freckle in sight. One tiny mole sat to the right of her mouth.

And that tumble of hair, clipped back, but determined to flood over her left shoulder, getting in her way. "You look better."

She sent him a sassy smile, teasing. "Which means I looked horrid before. Thank you!"

He mock-scowled and then laughed. "You know what I mean."

Her smile matched his. "I do, and I appreciate your concern. Some smells get to me, and that's what happened when we walked by The Pelican's Nest. I got caught by surprise."

Fresh-cooked bacon and sausage with a side of home fries. That was the exhaust scent on any given morning outside the restaurant. He'd been passing that diner for over a dozen years, and the breakfast smells on a cold winter morning? Temptation itself. But not for everyone, it seemed, and that made him wonder what kind of food folks ate in the Adirondacks.

He moved back where he needed to be and teased, "Life as I know it might come to an abrupt end if the smell of cooking bacon made me sick. Meat—it's what's for dinner."

"You're talking to a fellow carnivore, ninety-five percent of the time. Hopefully it won't happen again. I'd be okay with that."

He picked up the to-go mug of coffee he'd grabbed at Tina Marie's and sipped it, scalded his tongue and frowned. "Ouch."

"We've got coffee," she reminded him. "You don't have to buy coffee on your way over here."

"I could have made it at my place, too." He nodded toward the east-facing window as he picked up his measuring tape and pencil. "But I like to give Tina whatever business I can. She's a great gal."

"I can't disagree," Gianna said. "She's straightforward and down-to-earth. She told me she was raised working in a restaurant and by the time she got out of high school, she knew exactly what she wanted to do."

"From the beginning," he added.

She swiveled in her sewing chair and looked up, surprised. "And you know this because?"

"We were raised together. Went to the same school, although she's younger. And she and Max dated for years. Max is my youngest brother," he explained as he tested the wall for proper placement.

Gianna scooted the wheeled sewing chair closer, eyes wide. "Tina and a big, blond, bruiser Campbell? What a fun mix."

Seth sent her a look that said she was way off course. "Max is dark-haired, dark-eyed, about five-ten and totally Latino. But nice try. My parents had four kids biologically, then adopted three more. Max, Cass and Addie are adopted, but they're one hundred percent Campbell. Despite the difference in looks."

"That's awesome, Seth. And I love stories of unrequited love. What woman doesn't?"

"You're romanticizing Max's stupidity. He let her go. But that's a story for a different day."

"Or not at all, because Tina would probably like us to respect her privacy," Gianna replied. "I like it when folks offer me that option. I didn't realize Tina was from Kirkwood, though. Because the only restaurant around is—"

Seth nodded east as realization widened her eyes. "The Pelican's Nest. Her parents owned it. She worked there until she was twenty, when they sold it to her aunt and Tina was told her services were no longer needed."

"Whoa. Harsh."

"Her father hadn't foreseen that. His sister had promised to make Tina the manager. Tina would have had the job she loved and he'd have retirement money. Didn't work out that way. And that came on the heels of her breakup with Max. When your boyfriend dumps you for a slot in Special Ops as an Army Ranger, it's a fairly obvious breakup. I'm not gossiping. I'm sharing history."

The sympathetic curve of Gianna's mouth said she was in Tina's corner one hundred percent, but then she surprised him by saying, "That had to be rough. I wonder if it was just as rough for him. Does he have a new girlfriend? Did he get married?"

"We went from privacy to twenty questions. Quite a jump, Gianna."

"It's not disrespectful to ask the obvious." She adjusted the material beneath the needle and walked the machine through the thicker fold, one stitch at a time. "So does he?"

"Not that I know of, but he hasn't been home for a few years. And he's not a letter writer. He calls Mom once a week to check in."

"The family rogue. A wanderer. An adventurer. Every family's got one."

"Then that would be Max." Seth stood back, surveyed the finished look and began stowing his supplies.

"You're done?"

"For today."

"Oh."

A man could read a lot into a single syllable expression like that, Seth knew. Or he could pretend oblivion, put things right and go on his merry way.

Chin down, she kept working the material through the presser foot, inch by tedious inch. "Unless…?"

"Hmm?" She looked up, and the light in her eyes, a light she doused quickly so that he wouldn't see, said plenty.

"Unless you need me to stay." He crossed the room and crouched next to her machine so her face was quite close. "Want me to stay."

"I… Umm…"

He grinned, used the curve of his index finger under her chin to close her mouth and then stood. "Gotta get home. But I'm glad you weren't in too big a hurry for me to go."

He didn't wait for a reply, but he didn't rush out the door, either. He'd let her think about all the snappy repartee she could have shot back at him at her leisure, but as he let himself out the kitchen door, he caught a sideways glimpse of her through the shop window.

And she was smiling.

CHAPTER FIVE

*W*OMEN'S HEALTH SERVICES OF KIRKWOOD *Lake.*

Gianna studied the sign, then pulled open the heavy door. Excitement and reluctance battled inside her. So did the twins, as if sharing her anxiety.

Starting a relationship with a new doctor wasn't easy, especially mid-pregnancy. She hung her coat in the broad office closet and eyed the divided waiting room. One half teemed with young mothers and an assortment of small children around an interactive play area. The other side held older women for the most part, and she wondered if it was chance, choice or noise level that pushed the older clientele to the right.

The sprawled-out play area and easy-clean tile floor were two reasons for the young mothers to turn left. She approached the desk and gave her name.

The woman behind the counter smiled up at her. "You filled out everything online, I see."

"So much easier that way, right?" Gianna met her smile and the woman nodded.

"I agree. Have a seat and Wendy will be along to do your bloodwork shortly."

True to word, Wendy came for her a few minutes later. She checked vitals, weight, and when she assembled a series of tubes, Gianna drew a breath. She didn't love blood work, but she'd had enough of it over the years to be resigned to it. She breathed easy while they pulled multiple vials of blood from her arm, then waited as she pressed a gauze pad to the needle mark.

"Mrs. Costanza?"

She almost didn't turn. It wasn't until the nurse called the name a second time that Gianna stood. "I'm here."

"Good." The nurse smiled and extended her hand. "I'm Natalia Forrest, and I'll walk you through your appointment today. You're new to us, and this office can get a little manic—" she cast a smile to the kid-friendly area of the waiting room "—so if you feel you need to ask a question or have a quiet moment, just let me know."

Did this young woman have any idea how her words calmed Gianna's nerves? Most likely not, but her presence and her confidence-inspiring spiel meant Gianna wasn't the only nervous first-time mother they'd had.

"Come right in here, sit down and the midwife will be right in."

"Okay."

She should have brought Grandma along. Carmen had offered, but a do-it-herself streak had reared its head and she'd put her off. If she couldn't have Michael, she wouldn't have anyone.

Right now, facing this next step alone, she wished she'd chosen differently.

"Mrs. Costanza?" A woman stepped into the office from an anteroom to the left. "I'm Julia Harrison, the nurse-midwife."

Gianna put out her hand. "You're related to Zach?"

The midwife smiled. "You know my brother?"

"Not well. My grandmother and I are making vintage uniforms for him and Seth Campbell."

"You're Carmen's granddaughter."

Gianna shouldn't have been surprised that her

grandmother was already well-known throughout the town. "Yes."

"Nice to meet you. I met Carmen at Tina Marie's, and we had a great chat, which may keep me from locking up my two boys until I send them off to college. Amazing what five minutes of adult conversation will do."

Julia's normalcy relaxed Gianna more. "My grandmother has a knack."

"Yes." Julia took a seat and tapped the chart in front of her. "So. Are you scared to death?"

Emotion shifted upward. "Yes and no. Yes, because this wasn't supposed to happen this way. Me. Here. Pregnant and single."

Julia made a sympathetic noise but just nodded.

"No, because my other choice was to abandon these babies as frozen embryos." She looked down, breathed deep and brought her gaze back up. "So here I am, pregnant with twins."

Julia's expression reassured her. "I've got the records they shared from the fertility clinic and the original OB report from Adirondack Medical, but I'm going to start from the beginning if you don't mind. A full workup, tummy check, and we'll schedule your twenty-week ultrasound."

"You don't need one earlier than that?" The thought that she could just move ahead and have a normal pregnancy from such abnormal beginnings seemed unlikely.

"As long as everything looks normal, from this point forward you're like any other expectant mother. Except you're carrying twice the load. Alone."

Gianna sighed and shrugged. "Well, that got taken out of my hands, so right now it's just me and Grandma."

"And the town of Kirkwood," Julia told her. "I haven't been here long myself, but this town isn't afraid to rally around their own. New and old."

Like Seth, Gianna thought. And his mother. Tina and the reverend. They'd gone out of their way to make her and Grandma feel at home and involved.

Of course, keeping Grandma uninvolved was next to impossible.

"I'll see you in a few minutes. And, Gianna?"

Gianna turned, expectant. "Yes?"

"Welcome to Kirkwood."

Seth hit the hands-free button on his dash and waited for someone to answer as the system dialed Zach's cell phone. "Zach, you home?"

"Yeah. What's up?"

"Can I take ten minutes to go over the plan I've got for a couple of bicentennial things?"

"I drove to Barrett's Orchards to get apple fritters the minute they opened the doors this morning, so yes. Come on over. We'll feed you, if you hurry." His intentional stress on the last phrase told Seth that Piper was right there, listening. "I think Piper's on her third. Possibly fourth."

Seth laughed. "I'll be right there."

Piper Harrison pulled the side door open for him a few minutes later, and Seth wasn't surprised to see a fritter in her hand. "Is that really number four?" he teased as he stepped in.

"Three," she confessed, then shut the door. "I keep telling myself they're small, but I should probably figure out my own personal quantitative easing when it comes to food these days. And my husband isn't nearly as funny as he thinks he is."

"This is better than seeing you sick," Zach told them both as Seth moved into the warm kitchen. "Seth, you want coffee?"

"No. Gotta sleep, then shovel. Again." He handed Zach

the papers he'd carried in. "I can email this stuff to you in its final form, but I wanted to go over these two events." He tapped the information for the Founder's Day parade, the event that had inspired the town to dress them up in old-time gear. Then he indicated pages about the lakeside communities' famous annual Sidewalk Sale, an event that ringed the lake and included several villages. At the height of the summer tourist season, this event drew people from the entire Western New York Region and upper Pennsylvania, but this year they'd added a new component to the event with real-life demonstrations at historic sites.

Keeping traffic moving on the interstate was no problem. But once folks veered onto the two-lane roads linking the lakeside villages? Whole different story.

"I've been thinking about how to make the Sidewalk Sale traffic flow more organized, too, but I've got nothing." Zach crossed his arms over his chest and frowned. "If we had more parking…"

Summertime parking was at a premium in their waterfront communities, but for a big event like this, the problem became magnified.

"If it were a stationary event we could shuttle folks in from the high school." Seth aimed a look at the quick outline he'd drawn. "For the Around-the-Lake Sidewalk Sale that would mean multiple shuttles in varying directions."

"Not if you make everything one-way going clockwise around the lake for the weekend," Piper inserted.

"One-way? You're kidding, right? Convincing our locals they can't turn as desired? We'd be strung up for even suggesting that."

Piper made a face at her husband and shook her head. "The old folks love this year-long bicentennial celebration, and they all know that if you get stuck in your driveway on Sidewalk Sale weekend the long-range benefit to the town is worth it. And people clear out by five in the afternoon and don't come around again until nine the next morning, so it's only an eight-hour window."

"Eight hours of torture," Zach interjected.

Seth grinned. Piper rolled her eyes and didn't show her husband anything close to sympathy. "Arrange to have school bus shuttles from the high school like you suggested, only instead of going to one destination, they go to three—A, B and C. That way the three different villages are taken care of. Folks can hop off from village to village, see the lake, not fight the traffic, and you could make the right-hand lane bus-and-right-turn-only so folks in the left-hand lane could navigate more easily."

"That could actually work." Seth raised an eyebrow to Zach. "We'll have to figure out the details, and we'd need to barricade all left turns—"

"Except at a few designated exit points," Zach mused. "And use the auxiliary police to make sure the barricades are respected…"

"Which would keep Han Solo out of our hair for three days."

The two men exchanged grins. "Han Solo" was their name for an old-timer whose love of "Star Wars" meant wearing various Han Solo costumes throughout the year. Currently he was honoring winter by sporting the futuristic movie's ice planet episode, making Han Solo's fur parka a mainstay around town.

"My new neighbor is making him a new replica outfit," Seth told them. "They were mulling material for the vest while I was updating the shop lighting the other day."

Piper reached for a fourth fritter, slapped her own hand and sat down. "I saw your tenant at the doctor's office yesterday."

"Yeah?"

She nodded as she scanned his initial patrol plans, then looked up. "She doesn't know me, so I didn't accost her the way I usually do."

Zach snorted, holding back a laugh. Piper wasn't known for her low-key personality.

"She was coming out as I walked in."

"And you're all right? Everything's fine?" Seth asked.

"So far so good." Piper's face took on that strange, funny maternal look that hinted a greater understanding of life and the world in general. "I wonder if we're due around the same time."

"Due?" Seth stared at her, hard, as comprehension dawned. "You think Gianna's expecting? She can't be. She's—" He was about to say "single" but then realized he really didn't know a thing about Gianna's marital status except that she didn't wear a ring. Therefore single, right?

Obviously not. Unless Piper was mistaken.

She read his face and held up her hands, palms out. "All I know is what I see. She was carrying the little bag of things they give expectant mothers on their first-time visit, but maybe they do that for other procedures, too."

Seth doubted that. And while Piper's observation surprised him, it made perfect sense, too. The aversion to coffee. The smell of meat making her sick. The solicitous way Carmen looked at her, took care of her.

But if Gianna was here and pregnant, then somewhere there was a father, pushed out of the picture. Did he know Gianna carried his child? Did he care?

Fatigue wrapped itself around Seth's brain. Piper's observation gave him plenty to think about, but right now none of it made sense. Six or seven hours of sleep would take care of that, he hoped. He said his goodbyes, headed for home and parked in the upper end of his driveway. But as he trudged toward the house through the steadily falling snow, he glanced across the street.

The lights in the store glowed softly through the front windows, which meant Gianna was there, with Carmen, working. Setting up displays, unpacking goods, sewing vintage-look clothing.

Gianna. Pregnant?

His heart didn't want to believe it. Suffering the loss of Tori made him appreciate a father's role, a role he'd undertaken gladly for several years.

Now?

Every child deserved to have a mother and father, as God willed. His heart might not want to accept the fact of Gianna's condition, but he'd seen the evidence over the past few weeks and knew Piper was most likely correct. Gianna was pregnant, and alone. And right now there was very little that could make that right in Seth's book.

"Should we stop taking special orders once summer draws near?" Gianna asked Carmen the following week. "And how many people should we hire for summer help? And when should we start doing interviews?"

Carmen didn't look up as she "walked" her sewing machine needle around thick layers for the Han Solo vest. "We should cut down on special orders, perhaps, but I can keep sewing throughout the summer. You will be busy with the babies. We will hire help for the store, and I will be right here, sewing. So if extra help is needed, I am available," she finished, eyes trained on the fleece-lined garment.

"You're talking some long hours, Grandma," Gianna scolded. Her grandmother wasn't young, but she was the youngest septuagenarian Gianna had ever met.

Carmen waved off the warning. "When you come to a land of plenty as a child you appreciate much. Long hours, bah. I will be in my glory, meeting folks, sewing and seeing our dream come to life in this pretty community.

Have you asked Seth about painting the extra bedroom?"

She hadn't seen Seth to ask him, and it seemed a silly thing to call about when he lived across the street. He'd been working day and night. She knew that because his windows were visible from her kitchen. And whether he was there or not, his yard and drive were lit up each night, breaking the veil of darkness. The flow of light gave his gambrel-roofed Dutch colonial look welcoming. The old-fashioned front porch invited company to step up. Sit. Stay awhile. She could imagine a spread of red geraniums flanking the porch, catching the summer sun. And hostas beneath the thick-trunked deciduous trees shading the yard.

It was a lot of house for a single guy, so most likely Seth Campbell had a story. Something that caused the ache in his eyes when he gazed across the lake. The way he'd stop now and again to scan the road leading into town.

But Gianna had her own story to write at the moment, and her focus was self-centered: to bring this pregnancy to a successful conclusion. Hearing two heartbeats at the doctor's office the previous week? Music to her ears. She kept working as she answered the question about Seth and paint. "I haven't seen him, but I'll ask when I do."

"I've got that fresh batch of iced lemon bread on the counter," Carmen suggested. "Take him a loaf when he's home and ask about the painting. The fumes might make you sick as you get further along…."

"I hadn't thought of that," Gianna admitted. "I was thinking we could just open the windows in spring and the paint smell would be fine."

"Once the air gets humid, you extend drying time," Carmen reminded her. "I always liked to paint in the winter because the heat from the furnace makes things dry quickly, but I want to do whatever keeps you comfortable."

Gianna got up, crossed the room and hugged her

grandmother. "You are a treasure. I don't know what I'd do without you these last years, but especially now."

"And your mother will be less than pleased that I knew your secret and didn't tell her." Carmen met Gianna's gaze. "We will both be in big trouble, but it is worth it because what you're doing is noble, Gianna. Difficult, but noble."

"I am making things as right as I can," Gianna corrected her. "Nobility has nothing to do with it, Grandma. And as long as I've interrupted my work, I think I'll take your suggestion and run a loaf of bread across the street and check on the painting. I think a pretty yellow would be a good base coat, don't you? Maybe trimmed in greens and blues?"

"A cheerful nursery filled with love. Yes." Carmen waved her on. "And tomorrow we have been invited to the Campbells' house for Sunday dinner. I said yes. I hope that is fine with you?"

They needed to connect with people within the villages and the outlying areas. Gianna understood the importance of weaving themselves into the fabric of the town. Networking in small communities was more crucial than a big-city venue because small towns had a limited clientele. So yes, getting to know Seth's big family was a good thing. "His mother has been very nice."

Jenny Campbell had made it a point to stop by a couple of times, chatting before she went on her way. Gracious, fun and attractive, the petite woman made folks smile in her presence. Like her son, Gianna realized, because as she walked up his wide, sloping driveway, the thought of him made her smile. But when he swung open the broad back door and saw her, he didn't look pleased. Chagrined, maybe? Or annoyed.

But why? Realizing she knew little about her neighbor, she powered her ego with a deep breath and extended the foil-wrapped loaf. "Grandma sent this over. It's her famous lemon bread. I think you'll like it."

He eyed the loaf, then her. Angst and something else pressed his mouth into a hard line. He worked his jaw, rubbed a hand to the back of his neck and seemed trapped.

Which was beyond ridiculous, because she came across the street carrying a loaf of bread, not a marriage proposal. Gianna took a step back. "Look, I'm sorry if the bread offends you. It's really pretty good, but I'll tell Gram you're going low-carb for a couple of weeks to get into shape."

His expression didn't look one bit friendlier after her barbed remark. "I'm in shape, so she's not likely to believe that."

"Well, one can never be too careful." She pulled her coat tighter around herself, knowing she'd fit into it only for a matter of weeks. She'd had to start wearing maternity pants the past few days. Her old trick of expanding the waistband of her normal pants by looping a pony-tail band through the eye and around the button wasn't working any longer.

"You'll 'pop' faster with twins," Julia had advised. Less than two weeks later the babies proved her right. Right now she was hoping her coat would button…at least on top…until the end of February. But at this rate she might not make Valentine's Day. In the hill country that could make for a long, cold end-of-winter.

"You're cold, come in here."

That wasn't about to happen. Gianna took another step back, ready to end the disastrous conversation. "No worries, home is just across the street."

"Give me the bread, Gianna."

She sent him a look that could have frozen the Arctic, because that was about how her toes felt at that moment.

Cramped, cold and unprepared for standing on the snow-dusted step at his side door. "You don't have to take it, it's all right. Yes, it will hurt Gram's feelings, but—"

Seth reached out, grabbed her hand and unceremoniously ushered her into the house. "Up." He pointed up the four steps to his first floor, and she had little choice because six-foot-plus of square-shouldered, rock-jawed Campbell stood between her and the door.

"I have to get back. Gram's expecting me." Gram was doing no such thing, but the last thing Gianna intended to do was deal with her neighbor's grumpy mood. She'd come over to make a reasonable request of her landlord.

Right now? She was bound and determined to head home and paint the room herself.

"She knows where you are." Gianna's reaction said Seth's gruff tone hurt. The set of her chin compounded his reasoning. And that made him feel worse, to make a pregnant woman feel bad. What was the matter with him? It wasn't as if what she did mattered to him.

But it did. Kind of. And it probably mattered to some poor schmo who had no idea she'd gone off to start a new life carrying his child.

You're assuming. You're a cop; you know first-hand what assumptions do. They generally wind up being wrong and making people look stupid. Ask the woman. You've got nothing to lose.

A part of him hated the truth in that, but as he stepped forward to talk to her, the phone rang. He saw the "unknown caller" read-out and snatched the phone off the cradle quickly. "Tori. Is that you? How are you, honey? I miss you."

Gianna set the loaf of bread on the counter and slipped back through the kitchen door, down the stairs and into the frigid, thin afternoon light.

He stared after her, knowing he'd messed up, but Tori's soft voice held him in place. "I want to come home, Daddy. I just want to come home. Please?"

His throat seized. His gut twisted. Emotion made him grip the phone with unnecessary vigor. "I want that, too, honey. Is your mother there?"

"No." Again the whisper. "But her boyfriend is, and he won't be happy if he catches me on the phone."

Helplessness put a chokehold on Seth's voice. "I'd love to have you here, Tori. You're my little girl. You'll always be my little girl, my sunshine."

A thin strand of silence stretched the moment, but then he heard the old familiar tune they shared, only this time her voice wasn't full of childhood joy. This time her words were tiny and whispered as she avoided discovery by her mother's current boyfriend. The familiar words came out uneven as she sang "You Are My Sunshine."

He whispered back, repeating the old lyrics. But when he started into the verse about how much he loved her, a choked-back sob on her end broke the next familiar line and his heart. Again.

God, if You can hear me, if You can hear her, please look out for her. Guide her to safety, give her mother compassion and grace to seek what's best for her child. Dear Lord, Father God, hear the plea of Your son and daughter and bring my baby back home to me. Please.

He couldn't sing the last phrase, the final lament too dear to his heart. He paused, waiting to hear her voice, then realized the line had gone dead.

He hit the call-back code.

Nothing. She'd blocked it again, and that meant she was sure to get into trouble if Jasmine knew she'd contacted him.

He stared at the phone, hating it. Yes, he wanted contact with her, but not like this. Dear Father in heaven, not like this, tiny furtive seconds as if the love of a father for his child was wrong.

She's not your child, *his conscience reminded him.* If she were, you wouldn't be in this situation. It was foolishness and lack of foresight and follow-through that created this situation. And that falls at your doorstep. Nowhere else.

Child of his heart if not his blood.

He set the phone down tenderly, as if treating it with care would ensure Tori would find a similar fate. But the fear in her voice...

The heightened note of worry...

Made him suspect that wouldn't be the case. If there was evidence of a crime, he could pull out the stops and use the resources of the sheriff's department to begin a new search, but until he knew otherwise, the law was on Jasmine's side, all because he hadn't pushed for the adoption the way he should have. And that made him feel like a first-class heel.

CHAPTER SIX

"I WONDER IF HE SLEEPS."

"Who?" Gianna turned toward the kitchen early Sunday morning and caught the gist of her grandmother's speculation as she spotted Seth shoveling his driveway with more speed than should have been humanly possible. "Why do you say that?"

"I was up in the night to take my pills and his lights were on. And here he is, shoveling our drive and his before church. He must be plumb worn-out, is all."

"Your lemon cake either revived him or made him sick," Gianna supposed.

Carmen sent her a tart look. "Or life is throwing him curves, same as it does to most."

Gianna wasn't about to buy into that excuse for the guy's gruff behavior the previous day. He'd gone from flirting with her—which she didn't want, need or enjoy…although she *had* enjoyed it, she admitted to herself, and that felt wrong under the circumstances—to making her feel unwelcome at his door. No matter how good-looking and clean-cut the guy was, he had a chip on his shoulder, and drama was the last thing on her wish list for a snowy Sunday. Maybe he wouldn't be at his parents' home that afternoon. Maybe he was working a Sunday shift.

Better yet, a double.

His absence would leave her in peace to think and pray about the choices she'd made over the past six months. Choices that made her feel ridiculously good one moment and perched on the brink of tears the next, so whatever Seth Campbell's issues were, he could keep them to himself, and they'd both be better off for it.

She forced a slower pace for Gram's sake as they walked the two blocks to the historic hillside church overlooking the frozen lake. Two weeks ago Seth had made it a point to walk with them. Sit with them. Right now she was hoping he'd made his peace with whomever Tori was and that they'd be wonderfully happy together forevermore because the last thing she wanted in her life was another policeman.

The fact that the policeman seemed quite okay about not pursuing a relationship with her left a nasty internal scar on her ego.

Seth pulled into his parents' drive late that afternoon. He'd been tempted to skip the traditional gathering, but the big game was today and his mother had a knack for handling a crowd of football-loving family and friends for the early February tradition. And since his favorite team hadn't made the play-offs, much less the championship, he really didn't care all that much, but his family did. Once a Campbell, always a Campbell.

Parked cars lined the road's edge. Three familiar little faces screeched his name from the door as he approached the house.

"Uncle Seth!"

"He's here, Grandma! He came!"

"Uncle Seth, I've missed you this much, and look!" One of the twins—Dorrie, he realized as he drew closer and saw the tell-tale purple ribbon in her wavy dark hair—was now sporting a gap in the center of her mouth.

"You lost a tooth?" He stooped low, examined the tiny space and hugged her tight. "Did you find money under your pillow this morning?"

"Oh, yes." She hugged him back and whispered in his ear, "And Mommy says I'm not to brag about it because Aiden's teeth are just starting to wiggle, and Sonya's aren't wiggling in the least little bit so she kind of feels bad."

Little-kid speak.

The soft breath of a child at his ear.

The lofted excitement in her attempt to whisper.

All of it made him think of Tori. He'd prayed all night, then again this morning. He'd circled the lake and gone to the early service at Bemus Point, not wanting to face family and friends quite yet. Would he ever heal? Would he ever get to a place of comfort?

Yes, with God's help, but today had been hard. So hard.

"Seth!" His mother shooed the children back inside, scolding. "Guys, you're freezing us out with the door wide-open like that. Hustle up. Get back in there and let me close this door and hug your uncle. He looks like he could use a hug, good food and great company. All of which he'll find here if you actually let him through the door."

Sonya peeked up with a sweet smile for him. Aiden high-fived him then raced off to tackle his father in the main living room. Seth kept Dorrie in his arms, safe and sound, relishing the feeling. "Smells good, Mom."

Her expression said she read him like an open book. She always had. She blinked back sadness and touched his face. Just that one, simple caress. She knew. She cared. She prayed daily. He had to believe that somehow, someway, those prayers would be answered.

"Dorrie, would you take these chips out to the front room, please?"

"Sure!"

Dorrie wriggled out of Seth's grasp, grabbed the bowl

of chips and dashed to the front as fast as she could in case anyone was in danger of starvation.

His mother started to say something, but he shook his head. "Not now, okay? Let's focus on football for the moment."

"Football it is." She handed him a warm casserole of cheese-and-artichoke dip. "We'll lose ourselves in hot food, a good game and great conversation."

It sounded doable to Seth, until he turned the corner leading into the sprawling family room and ran into Gianna.

"Oh. Sorry." She looked flustered, and he wasn't sure if it was because of their awkward meeting yesterday or if she'd been hoping he might not show up. Probably both. "I didn't see you."

"My fault." He eased by her, wondering why his mother saw fit to invite strangers to a family gathering. As he set the dip onto the table near the sectional, an embroidered wall hanging drew his attention. "Whatsoever you do to the least of my people…"

He needed to grasp a bigger helping of his mother's Christianity because his was clearly lacking. He turned, determined to be nice because he had no reason to *not* be nice, and the first thing he spotted was Gianna's pale face as she wrinkled her nose. A sheen of sweat broke out on her upper lip. Her throat contracted. Without a word, Seth took her arm and steered her up the stairs, away from the game-day mix of foods. "Sit right here. I'll get you some crackers."

She didn't argue, and he considered that a minor victory. He grabbed plain crackers just as Piper and Zach came through the door with Zach's father and his two young nephews.

"I know that look." Zach commiserated as he put a gentle hand on her shoulder. "But I'm sorry you're still going through it. Piper got better about a week back."

Gianna flashed Piper and Zach a weak smile of acknowledgment. "Twins."

Two babies. With no father in the picture. Seth's heart did a funny twist in his chest.

"Really?" Piper sank onto the sofa alongside Gianna and grasped her hand. "Twice the fun, and work, but we won't dwell on that aspect of it right now." She lay a hand atop her belly. "I'm due Independence Day. How about you?"

"Two weeks earlier. So I'm sewing like crazy now because I'm going to be really busy come summer."

Seth heard the conversation. His brain registered the words, but what he wanted to hear was what had happened to the father of these babies.

Why did people consider fathers an inconsequential part of their children's lives these days? His pulse thrummed higher in his veins. The headache he thought he'd squelched hours ago started inching up his spine.

He moved to go back downstairs but stopped dead as Piper went straight to the point in typical style. "You're doing this alone, Gianna? Oh, honey, that's hard. I'm so glad your grandmother's here. I helped raise those two." She jutted her chin toward the porch, where Dorrie and Sonya were busy building a Lego castle with Aiden, Martin and Connor. "And I don't know how I would have done it without their grandmother around."

"Gram's amazing." Gianna made a face of chagrin. "Unfortunately my choices were limited. I'm a widow, so these guys have me and only me. And a whole lot of prayer."

A widow.

Seth's first reaction was remorse. How could he have thought the worst about her? Why would he jump to a conclusion like that?

But common sense made him rethink the situation. Timing made her explanation implausible. She didn't fit the profile of a grieving widow. She'd been in town for a month and she was due in five months.

The impossibility of that equation grated on his nerves. Was she lying? Covering something up?

Or did she not care that her husband had died?

Impossible, he decided. No matter what else, Gianna held raw emotion in her expression, her sweet smile. But Seth was a cop first. When things didn't add up, it was usually because someone fudged facts to fit the case.

"I'm so sorry." Piper took one of Gianna's hands in both of hers. "If there's anything you need, or you just want to talk to someone going through the same thing, call me. I'm only minutes from the village, and our winters can be cold, long and lonely."

"Thank you."

"But don't call us if you need help with the nursery," Zach drawled. "Because we can't seem to make up our minds on what room or what color. We decided not to find out if the baby was a boy or a girl, so we're mulling a ridiculous number of paint chips in random shades of green and yellow."

Piper made a face, but Gianna met Zach's gaze. "I actually went across the street to see Seth about painting the second bedroom upstairs a soft yellow. But we were interrupted and never got around to discussing it." She flicked a quick glance his way, as if unsure how to approach him about painting a bedroom because he'd been a first-class jerk.

She'd come to him, seeking help. Wanting advice. Maybe wanting a friend.

And what had he done?

He'd been cool and unreachable, then guilt-ridden because he knew his behavior was rude, and all because he assumed she'd given some guy the shaft.

A widow. With child. Trying to make it on her own. He'd need to do some up-front redemption with the

Holy Spirit because he'd jumped to conclusions and treated her badly, all because of his baggage with Jasmine.

He moved back toward the sofa, knowing he needed to make amends. "Gianna, would you like some tea? Mom's got that same stuff I've seen at your place."

"I'd love it. Thank you."

He read awkwardness in her gaze and realized she hadn't come to his parents' house prepared to explain her condition. The wave of sickness "outed" her, leaving little choice. But she'd handled the moment with a confidence that said she would do whatever proved necessary to make things right, and that was a mind-set Seth admired.

"And the truth shall set you free."

Was John's Gospel correct? Would truth offer an exit from the cloak of secrecy she'd worn for months?

Gianna prayed that would be the case as she opted away from the smells of the Campbell-filled family room. She'd hated lying to her family, keeping them in the dark about the treatments to prepare her body for these babies, but she'd picked her battles carefully.

She'd chosen silence because it was a rarity in the sprawling family. Various factions had opinions about everything. Family discussions were most often done at the top of their lungs, followed by food.

She crossed the Campbells' living room to study the array of family photos on the far wall. A host of Campbells smiled back at her, but her attention was drawn to three distinct siblings.

Clearly the Campbells hadn't looked for clones of themselves when they put out applications for adoption. One girl, tall and thin, sported milk-chocolate skin and thick, curly hair, much like Gianna's. The smaller woman, distinctly Asian, flashed an infectious smile at the camera in every pose, the kind of grin that invited laughter and repartee. And the single, dark-haired brother? Latino, tough, stern-faced and taciturn marked every picture but one. Someone had gotten a candid shot of him talking to his mother, and the look on his warm, smiling face said he loved Jenny Campbell with all his heart.

Other than that, the tough-guy gaze stayed firmly in place.

A small voice interrupted her perusal, and she turned. The twin with pink ribbons tiptoed up to her as the kick-off claimed most people's attention. "I made a little castle for my prince and princess. Would you like to see it?"

The child's peaceful gaze lightened Gianna's heart. As cheers for the underdog erupted from the sunken family room, Gianna stretched out a hand. "I'd love to."

She followed the child onto the heated front porch overlooking the lake. Darkness robed the grounds. From above the porch windows, streams of light spilled into the trees, but the lights could penetrate only so far. Beyond them lay snow and ice, inhospitable this time of year. She bent low and reached an arm around the girl's shoulders. "I love this. It's the perfect size for your little prince and princess."

"I know." The little girl whispered the words as if they were too special to say out loud. "This is Princess Stacey and Prince William. They're probably going to get married someday when Prince William comes back from fighting the horrible dragon." She held up a toy dragon designed to perch on a castle turret. "There's an army of little guys to defend the castle, and Uncle Seth lets us play with all of them."

She stressed the word *all,* but it was the other part of her phrase that made Gianna smile. "These are Uncle Seth's toys?"

A throat cleared behind her.

She turned, amused at the thought of the big, burly

policeman playing with miniature houses and villages. "It's nice that you share your toys with others. Very kindergarten-friendly."

"Yes. Well." Seth sat down on the porch rocker and raised a brow to his soon-to-be niece. "Since Sonya ratted me out, I must confess—I am a Lego-holic."

Sonya:pink ribbon. Gianna noted that for future reference because she couldn't discern a visible difference between the girls even though she'd tried every time they'd raced past her.

"He has tons of them at his house," explained Sonya. "But he brought a bunch over here for us to use."

"I've been collecting them since I was a kid," Seth explained. "Every Christmas and birthday that's all I wanted. Legos and zucchini bread."

"Not cake?"

He shrugged. "Never was much of one for frosting. But zucchini bread? I love it. And your grandmother's lemon cake was just as good."

His reference to yesterday's meeting made her wince inside. He seemed more relaxed now, but she wasn't in an emotional place to deal with anyone else's mood swings. Hers were quite enough for the moment.

"Now I watch for Lego sets on the internet," he continued. "Mom checks out garage sales for me. And so the collection grows."

"I think it's neat, Uncle Seth." Sonya slanted him a grin of pure admiration. "A lot of grown-ups forget how to play. You didn't."

He smiled, but veiled sadness weighted his eyes. "Sometimes it's hard to stay in practice. But I try."

"And that's good," Sonya decided. "May I come visit soon?"

"Yes. Check with Mom and Luke, okay? We'll figure out schedules. I'm working next weekend, but then you guys are off for winter break, so that would probably work."

"Cool!"

She ran off to tackle her parents for a definite date, and Seth took a seat on the rugged bench pulled up to the table. "Cute kid."

"Beautiful. So sweet and soft-spoken."

He laughed. "Well, Dorrie got enough noise factor for both of them, so they balance each other out. Sonya's quiet common sense keeps Dorrie and Aiden out of trouble. Some of the time."

Gianna smiled. "I love big families. I love being from a big family, even though I only have my brother. Most of the Bianchis live within three miles of our family home, so everything requires a family gathering. And family approval."

"Ouch. My mother's just the opposite, like one of those birds that pushes their young out of the nest with both wings flapping." He made a squawking bird sound while he did a mock shove with both hands.

Gianna burst out laughing, imagining the small woman shoving her big sons out the back door. "Sink or swim."

"Exactly. I still carry the bruises."

She made a face at him. "Poor baby. My mother can be a sweetheart, but she worries everything to death. Then she gets frantic, picks up the phone and calls friends, family and passing strangers to tell them what's going on and ask their opinion. By the time she's done she needs a heart pill and a coffee klatch so they can dissect our lives even further."

"But you love her."

Gianna smiled. "Oh, yes. She's been there for me through thick and thin. We lost my dad when I was young, and she managed to raise Joe and me on her own. With advice from Aunt Rose, of course, her slightly younger, slightly thinner sister. And Aunt Rose has been praying for me nonstop ever since I lost my husband. They're amazing women, very strong but crazy dramatic. I don't do drama well."

"Me, either. Aren't they worried about you being five hours away with these babies?"

Should she pretend they knew? Carry the pretense further? One look at Seth's honest face made her realize the time for honesty had come. "They don't know. Gram is the only one who knows I'm pregnant. It's a complicated story, but for the next few weeks I'm going to keep it quiet, because once I come clean there will be family everywhere. Right now I'm clutching the moments of calm and holding them close to my heart."

His face shadowed as he absorbed her information. He aimed his gaze outward, as if watching the water, seeing the waves, but the cold, frozen night allowed no such thing. Then he turned. His expression had relaxed but his eyes—"Campbell-blue" she'd named them when she'd seen his father's eyes of similar color—looked older. Troubled. "How hurt will they be?"

His question startled her. And made her think hard. Then she shrugged and met his look pragmatically. "They'll be hurt at first, but once they realize that I've moved forward, they'll be happy. I was..." She didn't know how to say this next, how much to explain, but something about Seth made it almost easy to share things she'd never told anyone. Although she hadn't exactly felt that way yesterday. "I went a little crazy after Michael died. There were times—" Her throat choked because thoughts of self-destruction didn't sit well in the midst of faith, family and friends. The mental anguish that swelled after losing her husband and child put a serious hurt on her, heart and soul. "—that I didn't want to live. I think I crawled under the covers and stayed in bed for a long,

long time. And even when I was pretending to be awake, my spirit stayed under those covers."

His face softened. "Grief's a heartbreaker."

"Yes."

"So." He stood and reached out a hand. "I know you haven't eaten a thing since you got here, and from the look of you, you're not eating enough for one these days much less for three people. How about my kitchen specialty? Campbell Grilled Cheese? Easy on the stomach, and my mother has homemade bread that makes the sandwich a meal."

Grilled cheese had never sounded so good before. Or was it the big guy's empathetic look? His calm gaze? The strength that came through the touch of his hand to hers? A strength she could lean into.

Except she didn't dare lean on anyone's strength but her own and God's. And certainly not another man wearing a badge and a gun. But when Seth's hand clasped hers and pulled her up, when they came face-to-face for just a moment, a tiny stretch of time that felt like it should last forever, a part of her wanted to stay right there, caught in the moment. Hand to hand. Heart to heart.

He tugged her forward and she went willingly, wondering what is was about this man that attracted her.

You want a list? Let's start with the good looks. The broad chest. The way he carries himself tall but thoughtful. That easy smile. The depth of character. The strong way he stands, legs braced—the wolf looking after the sheep. And if that's not enough for you, try the sweet nature that lies beneath the gruff exterior.

She'd had enough of the gruff exterior yesterday, but the rest of the list was spot-on. She perched on a kitchen stool and chatted with him as he put together a wonderful, thick grilled cheese sandwich. And when she took the first bite, she knew he was right—she'd never had a better grilled cheese. But part of that might be the company she kept in the kitchen, the calming effect of the man's ease. As a cheer erupted from the family room two levels down, she looked up at him, chagrined. "Seth. I forgot about the game. Go down and watch it," she ordered, sounding a lot like her mother. That thought made her cringe inside, but she didn't desist. "You're missing everything."

A slow smile worked its way across his face as he contemplated her, a smile that said maybe the game wasn't all that important, but being here was.

She was crazy to think that. Foolish.

But then he reached out one of those big hands and grazed her cheek ever so gently. "There's always another game."

Her heart went soft. His look. His touch. The warmth in his face alongside the pain he tried to hide.

She understood that ploy all too well.

She smiled up at him, determined to play nice but keep her distance. He didn't know her issues. He'd find out soon enough, because once her family arrived in town nothing would be kept secret.

She loved their honesty but couldn't handle the theatrics that went hand-in-hand, not just yet. For now she was content with her sewing and the feelings of a successful pregnancy to date. That was enough to thank God for at the moment.

Seeing Seth's profile as he washed up the griddle, humming lightly, a tiny longing grew inside her, a small, yawning hole of emptiness.

Michael should have been here caring for her. Helping her. Through no fault of his own he was gone.

But watching Seth make quick work of the kitchen chores, including washing up the dishes his mother had left behind, expanded that tiny window of hope. It felt good being here with Seth in the quiet of the kitchen.

Maybe too good, but she'd figure that out tomorrow. Right now, it felt right, and Gianna hadn't been able to say those words for a long time.

Tonight she could.

CHAPTER SEVEN

YESTERDAY HAD TURNED OUT MUCH better than he'd expected.

Seth mulled the big game party at his parents' as he steered his SUV along the winding road circling Kirkwood Lake after working the afternoon shift on Monday. And with every thought of family and football came a more intriguing image of Gianna.

He'd glimpsed the woman behind the story. Hurting. Toughened. Forged by life.

But he also saw the gentility in her decisions. Her time line was skewed, and Seth might not have gone through an actual pregnancy with Jasmine, but he had learned enough to know that science could perform some amazing feats these days. But that thought drew him up short, because shouldn't God be in command?

Yes. Which meant arbitrarily creating children for a one-parent home wasn't part of God's plan.

He pulled into the driveway, did a K-turn in the turn-around and stopped short when his headlights caught a person in the twin beams. Small. Long, brown hair. Probably frozen solid sitting on his back porch.

Tori.

He shoved the car into Park and leaped out in one motion. "Tori!"

"Dad?"

Her voice broke. Her eyes filled as he approached. The gleaming outside lights bathed the yard in welcome-home brightness. He grabbed her in his arms and held on tight.

His girl. His beautiful child. Back here, with him, tonight. "Honey, come in. Let's get you warm. How long have you been here? And why didn't you call me and tell me?"

He hustled her into the house, tossed a few extra logs onto the fire and then bundled her in blankets next to the woodstove.

She was shaking from cold. Tired and worn. But she was here, and they'd figure out the rest later. Right now he simply wanted to care for her.

And then he'd figure out what to do about Jasmine.

"How are we doing?" He brought her a mug of hot cocoa with marshmallows. "Careful, it's hot."

"Okay." She breathed over the surface of the drink, and her expression told him she was exhausted. Worn-out from the cold and who-knew-what-else.

"How'd you get here, honey?"

"Mom dropped me off."

"She dropped you off in the cold?" Callous, unfeeling, self-absorbed… Had she ever put Tori first?

No. And he should have recognized that years ago. Feeling his way, he gave Jasmine the benefit of the doubt. "She thought I was home?"

"Yes, well, the lights."

Thwarted by his own preparations, he knew exactly what she meant. He'd bathed the yard in welcoming light two years before, hoping and praying the light would greet Tori's homecoming someday. The fact that his good intentions went awry hit low. "Sorry. I wanted everything to be lit up for you when you came back. You know. Cheerful. Happy to see you."

She peeked a smile up at him, then leaned into his knee as she yawned.

And oh, that feeling. Having her there, leaning on him, seeking his support. The smile, the tiny glimpse of the dimple he'd missed so much.

His heart pressured the walls of his chest.

Could she stay?

Was Jasmine playing another one of her games? Was she going to show up here soon and reclaim her beautiful daughter?

Tori yawned again. She needed sleep. There'd be plenty of time for talking tomorrow. It was late, and as he walked her down the hall to her old bedroom, he ran a hand through his hair. "I don't have any clothes your size, honey. The stuff in here is more than two years old." He hit the light switch, and the pink-and-green room warmed in the glow.

Tears filled Tori's eyes. "You kept it the same."

She looked surprised and humbled. Seth bent low. "Of course I did. It's your room, Tori."

"But Mom said…" Her voice wavered. Her face gave him a glimpse of hardship and want. "I thought everything would be different. That you wouldn't want me anymore."

Anger knotted the base of his spine. Why would someone tell a child lies like that? To shush her? Make her stop asking about him, about coming home?

He bent low and locked his gaze with hers, speaking slowly and softly. "I will always want you, honey. You're my daughter, no matter what the legalities say. I rocked you, carried you, played with you and taught you how to roller-skate and ride a two-wheeler."

"And ski," she added.

She'd caught on to skiing like she was born to the slopes. He smiled and cupped her cheek with his hand. "This is your home, Tor. And it always will be. No matter what anyone says." He frowned at the dresser drawers. "But I don't have pajamas that will fit you. What's in your bag?"

She appeared surprised that she still clutched the ratty backpack in her hand. "Just my stuff."

Her stuff, her worldly goods, shoved into a threadbare backpack with plenty of room to spare.

But he wouldn't think about that. He'd focus on the here and now, the blessing he'd found at his door. The grace of Tori's return. They'd sort it all out after much-needed sleep. He went to switch off the light and a look of utter panic filled her eyes. "No, please. I can sleep with the light on, okay?"

His heart read her terror and he wanted to seriously hurt someone because no child should ever have to fear the dark. But he didn't want Tori to see his anger. He breathed deep, smiled and tucked her into bed, grubby clothes and all. "Then lights on it is, Pumpkin."

Her eyes filled with tears, but then they closed in slumber before the tears could escape. All but one, and that tiny tear snaked a path down her cheek.

Seth caught it on his finger, his heart sorrowed by whatever she'd endured, but blessed by her presence. He knelt beside her bed, grasping her hand in his, and let his soul sing a Psalm of thanksgiving, praising God with silent shouts of gladness. Seeing her there, sound asleep, wedged open a door to his heart he'd thought forever closed.

Light seeped through the cracks, hinting of possibility. For the moment he'd grasp that hope and run with it.

He called into work, explained the situation to the nighttime command and took a two-day emergency family leave to get things in order. Two days wasn't much, but with the department shorthanded, it would have to do. And if he got his wish, they'd have a lifetime to fix what had gone so terribly wrong. As long as Jasmine went along with it—and when it came to his former wife, that was never a given. Usually things came with strings attached, and Tori's sudden reappearance?

In this case the "strings" might be more like financial "ropes," but he'd been preparing for this opportunity since the day Jasmine had vanished with Tori. He'd scrimped and saved, getting ready to do whatever proved necessary to keep Tori with him.

He just prayed it would be enough.

He checked in on Tori. She was sound asleep. A deep sleep.

He called his parents straight off. "Mom? Tori's back."

"What?"

He felt exactly the same way. "I came home from work tonight and she was on the back step."

"In this cold? Are you kidding me? Who does that to a child?"

Mom had never been a big fan of Jasmine. Dumping your kid on a frigid, snowy night clearly hadn't raised her estimations of her former daughter-in-law. "She thought I was here because of the lights."

"Oh." His mother's voice calmed. She knew the reason he'd kept the yard lit up like an airport was to welcome Tori home someday. His plan had backfired, but Tori was safe and warm now. Here at home, right where she belonged. "She's got nothing so I need to take her shopping tomorrow."

"Wonderful! I'll come along if that's okay."

He laughed, feeling the first vestige of peace he'd known in years. "It would be if you were in town, but you're in Buffalo tomorrow for that hardware convention with Dad."

"Your father is perfectly capable of going alone."

Seth knew that. But he also knew that his mother was the Campbell with the uncanny knack for knowing what goods to push in season. What fads would pay and what would end up collecting dust in the back room. Therefore—

"I'll take her. If we get stuck I'll call you. Or we can go back Wednesday. I took two days off so I can get her enrolled in school."

"You're sure she's staying, son?"

He didn't miss the note of caution in his mother's voice, the tone that said Jasmine wasn't to be trusted. He'd learned that the hard way, but right now he had little choice. "I'm not sure of anything at the moment, but I'm going to get things in order assuming it will all work out. And school's a must."

"I can't wait to see her."

"I know. She's grown. She missed you a lot. If you've got Wednesday free, we can finish things up together then. I'll take my two best girls to lunch."

"Perfect!"

As he hung up the phone, Gianna's image came to mind, as if lunch wouldn't be complete without the petite, sassy Italian woman offering advice.

Having seen the goods now being displayed in her "old-world" store, he realized she had a knack for putting together a look. But her life appeared no more ordered than his, and he had enough drama and turmoil to last a lifetime. The last thing he wanted was more. And yet when he finally lay down to sleep, it was Gianna's face that drifted through his mind. Pretty. Saucy. Independent. And offering her life up for twin babies she was destined to raise alone. The kind of Solomon-esque sacrifice a true mother would make.

That thought made him smile as he dozed off.

"A different light this morning," Carmen mused as she puttered around the store just before dawn, setting up her sewing corner. "Upstairs, too. That's odd."

"What's odd is your fascination with our neighbor's sleeping habits," Gianna retorted. "Let's not be 'those' neighbors, okay?"

"I'm not." Carmen sent her a tart look. "But looking out for others isn't the same as being nosy. There's a fine line, my girl."

"Our family doesn't just cross the line, we steamroll it," Gianna reminded her as she glanced across the street. Their kitchen window offered a perfectly framed view of Seth's home.

Gram was right. The upper left-hand corner of the house had two windows, one facing south, one facing west. Both windows were lit, and she'd never noticed those lights on before.

Not that she'd looked, of course.

She fought a grumbling sigh, knowing she let Seth get too close on Sunday. Now she'd need to nip the attraction again. But the truth was, she didn't want to.

A conundrum. She was living multiple conundrums, mostly of her own doing, and she didn't need another, but the mellow glow of that upstairs light made her wonder what was going on....

And that curiosity was exactly the reason she'd gone into this pregnancy incognito. Because nosiness ran in her family, and she wasn't about to jump on the need-to-know bandwagon.

As daylight flooded the lakeside village, she couldn't shake the image of those corner windows, filled with light against the snow-crusted roofline. The Currier and Ives beauty of spilling lamplight made her smile, no matter what reason lay behind the soft glow. The heartwarming view made the cop who lived alone more of a mystery.

Minding her own business had become her mantra years ago. She decided she'd do well to re-embrace that mind-set now.

"I had to peek in and see if I was dreaming." Seth grinned at the tousled-haired girl tucked beneath the handmade quilt his mother had created for Tori a few years before. "And if this is dreaming, kid, I don't want to wake up."

"Dad." She reached for him, and he crossed the room quickly. Gathering her into his arms, he held her close, inhaling the scent of her. When he finally set her back down, he sank onto the bed next to her.

"Tell me again how you got here. Did your mother really drop you off, or did you run away?"

"She dropped me off," Tori began. She turned her face to the window, but not before Seth read the look within. She wanted to be here. He knew that.

But what she wanted more than that, and what she would probably never have, was the normal love of a mother willing to sacrifice for her child. Jasmine wasn't the sacrificial sort, as his mother had warned him years ago.

He hadn't listened. And if he had, where would Tori be today?

Where will Tori be tomorrow is the better question, his conscience cut in. You still have no legal right to keep this child. She's not yours and never was. Are you going to be stupid again?

No, Seth decided. He'd take this step-by-step and enjoy each day they had, because that would show Tori the meaning of true parental love, something he'd taken for granted as a kid. Now he realized the rarity of that daily sacrifice. "Did she give you a number where we can reach her? Did she sign the court papers I sent her last year?"

Confusion clouded Tori's features. "I don't know."

"No problem, kid. Why don't you take a shower while

I make a few phone calls, then we'll head to Clearwater and buy you some clothes."

"New ones?"

The hopeful look on her face wrenched his heart. "Sure."

"Oh, that would be so nice, Daddy."

Her face glowed with anticipation. She hurried to the bathroom, and while she was in there, he made several calls. If this drop-off was the answer to prayers, he needed to make the most of it as quickly as possible. And that meant locating Jasmine and getting her to make things legal, but Seth wasn't a fool in love any longer. Jasmine had a knack for looking out for herself, which meant she might disappear for a very long time. But in the meantime, Tori was safe with him, right where she belonged. And nothing could taint how good that felt right now.

"Nothing fits right." Tears threatened as Tori set the fourth pair of pants aside. "They're either way too long or not big enough to zipper."

Try as he might, Seth had no answers. Were girls really this hard to fit? Couldn't they just get a size ten like they used to and be done with it?

"No," his mother advised when he made a clandestine phone call while Tori tried on a dress. "Tori's at that in-between stage, so some things from the ladies department might fit and others from the kids department might fit. Or you can shop in juniors because she's petite."

Ladies? Kids? Juniors? Petite? His mother might as well be talking a foreign language.

"Why not call it a day and you and I can take her tomorrow," Jenny offered. "Or you could ask Gianna for help."

Gianna.

He'd watched her trim a large dress into one suitable

for her grandmother in a few hours' time. He'd seen her pull apart a sleeve, adjust it, put it back in place and create an entirely new "vintage" look for a pattern. Yes, Gianna or Carmen could help. He felt instantly better and tried to tell himself it was simply because Gianna knew her way around fashion and a sewing machine.

The fact that her wide brown eyes made him long to draw closer was academic. She was living choices from a life that had nothing to do with him.

So was he.

But she was a talented woman who plied her needles with an artist's touch. Surely she could make sense of a nearly twelve-year-old girl's wardrobe.

He hoped.

"Seth, hi." Gianna would *not* allow her heart to pitter-patter like some cute kid movie about happily-ever-afters. Been there. Done that. Clearly overrated. "What's up?"

"I need your help."

He sounded funny. Good, but different. She set her water glass on the counter and nodded as she eyed his house through the kitchen window. "I'm listening."

"My daughter has come home."

His daughter?

Seth had a daughter? No one had said anything about that, and in small towns, talk ran rampant. Or maybe that was just in her small town, because this one didn't seem to be quite as gossip-fired. "Seth, that's nice. You sound delighted."

"Thrilled, actually, but we're having problems with clothes and my mother suggested your help. She'd be here but she's in Buffalo with Dad. Do you have time, Gianna? If we get clothes that need adjustments, can you do that?"

"You took on shopping all by yourself? Seth, that's

either remarkably admirable or borderline insane. How old is your daughter?"

A moment of silence stretched long before he answered. "Nearly twelve."

Gianna laughed out loud. "I'm going with the borderline insanity theory in that case."

He sighed and in that soft breath she read the sensitivity of his gentle heart. "Mom offered to come back early, but I hated to make her miss this convention. And I thought we'd do okay shopping together."

"But—"

"Nothing fits right." He whispered the words as if trying to spare his daughter's feelings. "We're both getting discouraged, but we have to find something because she's got no clothes."

No clothes. Sudden reappearance. The light shining boldly through two previously dark windows.

Empathy flooded Gianna. Whatever this story was, she read the slight note of panic in Seth's voice and needed to help him. Wanted to help him. "Where are you guys?"

"At the mall in Clearwater."

"I'll be there in thirty minutes. And I'm pregnant and starving, so lunch first would be a very good idea."

He laughed, and the sound of that laugh, well-rounded and more relaxed, said he'd gladly feed her if she helped him figure things out. The fact that she was eager to help him was something she'd face later on. For the moment, a shopping trip at the opposite end of the lake sounded like a great excuse to leave her sewing chair for the afternoon.

"Gram? I'm heading down to Clearwater to help Seth shop for his daughter."

Carmen raised a brow of interest. "A change has occurred."

Her voice said she knew more than Gianna, but that wasn't a big surprise. Folks confided in Carmen, even those who didn't know her, and Carmen was the exception to the family rule. She wasn't afraid to keep things quiet and pray privately. It was a lesson some of her offspring should adopt more often. "So it seems. I won't be back for a while."

"I'm glad you're getting out." Carmen waved her toward the door. "Do not forget your scarf. Taking a chill is never good."

Gianna paused, retraced her steps, and bent to kiss her grandmother's cheek. "I love you, Gram. I don't know what I'd do without you."

"Ach." Carmen brushed off the warm emotion with a shrug and a smile. "You. Me. We are much alike. We have always known this. Go. Have fun. Retail therapy is a wonderful thing."

Retail therapy.

Gianna laughed on the way to the car because her grandmother was right. Spending a day shopping with Seth and his daughter—spending someone else's money—equated to great therapy. She loved her job, and the grand opening was drawing close, so the need to produce more vintage-looking goods pressed her to sit long hours at her machine, but this?

A day at the mall on a cold, clear February afternoon? A gift.

He wished he'd thought of this sooner.

As Gianna explained the size differences to a suddenly enthusiastic Tori, Seth realized he'd been over his head, possibly drowning in cotton-poly blends, for hours.

"So I should look for pants in juniors." Tori lifted a pair of size sevens and Gianna handed her two more sizes to try on. "And shirts…"

"Shirts might be in both," Gianna explained. "The thing is, some junior styles show a little too much skin, if you know what I mean. Of course, properly fit undergarments make the outfit, so why don't you and I go over there and spend some of your father's money."

Tori blushed at the mention of underwear, and Seth blessed Gianna's take-charge nature. He hadn't even thought of that when they started out because shopping for his little girl used to be so easy.

Not anymore.

He gulped and followed them. Once Gianna had Tori properly fitted, they moved back to juniors. Before he knew it, three pairs of jeans had made their way into his arms. Then two sweaters. Two hoodies. And three long-sleeved T-shirts with some kind of glittery designs across the front.

"Accessories," Gianna announced, and Tori nodded.

"Like cute earrings? Scarves?"

"Exactly!" Gianna led the way to a fun little store down the mall but managed to stop by two separate kiosks, where Seth parted with more of the current week's paycheck.

"This is cute, isn't it?" He paused by a window where a store mannequin sported a stylish short jacket, a great scarf and a rippled headband. "Tori, what do you think?"

"I love it, but it's expensive." The moderate price tag made her shrink back. Her expression told Seth more about the past two years than he cared to know.

"I actually have an almost identical jacket in the store for less than half that price, Seth." Gianna tipped her gaze up to his, and the moment she did, time slowed…

Then paused.

It paused for her, too. He saw it in her eyes, the soft intake of breath, the moment stretching into something beyond today.

She blinked, sighed, then turned her attention to Tori. "It's a size eight, but I think it would work for you, Tori.

And if we get the scarf here and use those cute boots we just bought—"

"The boots that are growing heavier as we speak," Seth reminded them, but he smiled as he said it, because he couldn't remember ever having this much fun on a shopping trip.

"Why don't you take those things to the car," Gianna advised him. "We'll go in here and buy this scarf, and that should just about do it for today, don't you think?"

"Pajamas."

"Oh." Gianna made a face. "I should have thought of that. Okay, Seth, meet us at Penney's and we'll make cruising the pj's section our last stop before we stop by The Cakery."

"After the lunch we had? Really?" She sent a deliberate look to her expanded waistline and he backed off instantly. "Sorry, should have thought first. Cake is imperative. My bad."

"I love babies." Tori smiled softly as she acknowledged Gianna's condition with a glance. "If I take a babysitting course this spring, can I maybe help you when the baby comes?"

"That's a marvelous idea," Gianna told her and she wrapped an arm around the shy girl in a quick hug. "And it's two babies, so I'll be needing help. If it's all right with your father, of course."

As if he had a choice. Seeing those two faces turned toward him, waiting for his answer, he had to nod, which meant he might have to practice saying "no" all over again. Right now, having Tori back in Western New York, all he wanted to say was "yes." "I like the idea of a babysitting course," he told them. "Money in the bank, kid."

"I'll save it for my first car," Tori announced, and the fact that she'd be able to drive in four years was another reality shock.

Tori wasn't a little girl any longer. The shopping trip from department to department made that apparent.

And she wasn't sure of herself. She'd been a self-confident child before she'd disappeared. Now she seemed shy and nervous, carefully picking what to say and do. Seth was well-schooled in victim mentality. He understood how victims would compromise as needed to stay safe. Stay alive.

That was what he saw in Tori, to a lesser degree. The relaxed and capable girl he'd helped raise had done as needed to stay off her mother's radar.

Or the boyfriend's radar. And that thought coiled Seth's anger deeper and tighter.

But time and God could provide great healing. He believed that, and he'd do whatever he needed for Tori to see that, too.

By the time they pulled into his driveway, his parents' car was parked in front of the garage.

"Tori!" His mother bounded from her car and grabbed Tori in a huge hug mingled with tears. "I'm so glad to see you. Oh, let me look at you!" She stepped back, marveled at how Tori had grown, then hugged her again.

"Jen, there is a perfectly good house we can do this in," Seth's father reminded them. "I'm gonna assume it's warmer than standing out here, too." But he stepped right up and took his turn hugging his beloved almost-granddaughter. "Tori, we missed you."

"Me, too, Grandpa."

A mix of emotions surged through Seth, but the sound of Gianna's motor pushed him to hand his mother the keys to the house. "You guys take the pizza in and get settled. I'm going to run across the street and thank Gianna again."

"Go right ahead, we've got all this stuff." Charlie grabbed hold of several shopping bags, Jenny retrieved the pizza and they made their way through the snow that had re-blanketed the sidewalk while they were gone.

Seth jogged down the driveway and across the village street. "Gianna?"

She turned toward his voice with a sack full of groceries, and when she did, his heart did a happy dance inside his chest. "Hey."

"Thank you." He drew close and smiled down at her, wondering how anyone's eyes could be so deep and dark and still shine so sweetly. "This shopping trip was destined for disaster until you came along. I owe you."

"You don't." She puffed a tuft of windblown hair from her eyes, but the stubborn lock resettled exactly where it had been, across her eye and cheek.

Don't do it.

He shouldn't. He knew it. She knew it. A mix of emotions darkened her gaze, and the slight intake of breath said she should step back. Break the moment. Ease away.

But she didn't, and Seth reached down to move the strand of hair back, behind her ear. The curve of his hand stayed right there, cradling her face, her cheek, the soft skin an invitation to linger.

"Seth, I—"

"I know." She couldn't, shouldn't and wouldn't, and because he felt the same, he understood, but his stubborn hand seemed quite happy where it was, tucked against the softness of her skin.

She flushed. Warmth stole beneath his palm despite the cold winter's day. She raised her chin, and the pain he read in her face, a sorrow that bit deep, said too much. "It's just—"

"I get it, Gianna." He smiled down at her but then gave his hand and her cheek a quick look. "But this might be beyond us. Beyond reason. So we might just have to go with it. See where it leads."

"It can't lead anywhere, Seth. Not ever." She did step away then. She turned her attention to his house and took another step back. "Go. Enjoy your daughter and your pizza. And thank you for a lovely afternoon."

She moved inside, not allowing him to get the door for her, and she didn't look back.

Not ever...

He heard the words. He read her gaze and the strength governing her intentions. She was right, too. He'd promised himself to avoid entangled situations after his disastrous marriage to Jasmine. He'd been careless about the legalities of parenting someone else's child, and he'd paid the price with two years of aching loss. And he was currently re-embroiled in the same situation. Tori was here, safe and sound, but she wasn't his legally, which meant he could be setting himself up for a fall all over again.

But as he retraced his steps up his drive, the curve of Gianna's cheek imprinted on his heart, he wasn't any too sure what to do about that, because staying away from her held no appeal whatsoever.

CHAPTER EIGHT

"WE HAVE ANOTHER CONSIGNMENT FOR the bicentennial." Carmen waved a scrap of paper like the gold ring at a carnival attraction. "Two more officers."

Gianna scrutinized the Grand Opening sign she'd been stenciling on a painted plywood board before turning. "Are they coming in soon, and do we need to order fabric?"

"Yes and no."

A pragmatic answer that revealed little. Gianna straightened up and walked away from the sign. Maybe it would look better if she absented herself for ten minutes and then looked with fresh eyes. "I'm confused."

"They're coming today, but they're women, and women officers didn't exist back then so we're outfitting them in period costume."

"Which period?" Gianna frowned. The thought of encumbering officers with clothes that could impede their progress during a problem didn't sit well. "We're not talking long dresses, are we? Because that's not only stupid, it's dangerous."

"You are correct, of course. I was thinking something along these lines." She handed Gianna two quick sketches she must have done that morning. "What do you think?"

"The halter-collar plaid shirt is great," Gianna told her.

"But I'm not a fan of the pants. What about a simple A-line skirt?"

"Or maybe breeches?"

"Yes." Gianna tapped the sketch with a finger of approval. "The pockets would allow room to keep a weapon. We're not putting cops on the street with no recourse if threatened."

"Because town celebrations are a dangerous enterprise." Carmen deadpanned the words, but her eyes said she understood.

"There's danger everywhere these days, Gram." Gianna stared outdoors and sighed. "Nothing is really safe, is it?"

"Was it ever, darling?" Carmen put her hand on Gianna's shoulder. "The Bible tells us story after story of anger and animosity. Jealousy. Greed. Man is as inclined to sin as the sparks to fly upward."

"Then how do you avoid it?" Gianna asked. She passed a hand across her rounded belly. "How do I even think to keep these babies safe in a world filled with risk?"

"We do our best. And we pray. And this is a nice town, safe enough."

"Nothing seems safe enough, Gram. Not anymore." Gianna whispered the words, wondering again if she'd done the right thing. Two babies would come to her in a few months' time. Was she strong enough? Stable enough? Quick enough to parent them both once they were old enough to dash off in separate directions?

Carmen interpreted the question behind the words. "Your options were guided by your faith and your belief in life, Gianna." She took Gianna's face between her strong and capable hands, hands that had shown Gianna so much in three short decades. "You chose life. Life is never a bad thing."

A knock sounded on the side door. Gianna hauled in a calming breath, planted a smile of welcome on her face and went to open the door.

Seth stood on the other side. Tall. Strong. Vigorous. And in uniform.

Her heart clutched and refused to let go.

She knew he was a deputy sheriff. But the visual of Seth in uniform, looking strong and defensive, solid and reliable, rooted her to the floor. She tried to move and couldn't.

"Gianna?" His voice held question and something else. Concern? Of course, because she must look woefully foolish, staring at him.

"Seth, come in. I wasn't expecting you because we already fit you. But I think I was expecting her." She shifted her attention to the young woman in a similar uniform, and the woman's bemused expression said she'd rather be anywhere else right now.

So would Gianna.

"Come in!" Carmen bustled their way, grabbed the woman officer's hand and led her into the well-lit shop area. "I am Carmen Bianchi, and this is my granddaughter Gianna Costanza. And you are?"

"Before I got told I needed to get trussed up in some kind of Barbie doll getup for this summer? I was Deputy Sheriff Nikki Peters. Now I'm not sure who or what I am."

Carmen laughed. "I do believe our Seth felt much the same way last month, but we will do everything we can to ensure your confidence, deputy."

The back door opened and another woman stepped in. She wasn't in uniform, but her grin said she'd overheard some of Nikki's spiel. "Make her wear a skirt, please. It will be the first time since her high school graduation gown."

"I outrank you, and I'm armed," Nikki reminded the other woman, but her shoulders relaxed. "Not a skirt, right? You wouldn't truss me up in something that impedes my job, would you?"

"No, ma'am." Gianna moved closer and handed her the sketch with the trousers crossed out. "Here's what we're thinking." She then added a computer printout of a pair of loose-fitting and stylish breeches. "This halter top, the little jacket if needed, depending on weather, and the breeches. That way you can carry your weapon and anything else you need concealed beneath the jacket. We'll make it lightweight and breathable so it won't be any heavier than a summer-issue uniform, but sized to be worn over Kevlar."

"Sign me up," declared the other woman. She shed her jacket and hooked it on Gianna's chair. "If Princess Nicola needs to go first because she's on duty, I can wait. Hey, Seth."

"Maura, how's it going?"

"I'm ready for spring. Mother Nature isn't. Same old, same old."

Seth laughed and tapped his watch. "Thanks for letting Nikki go first. We're on lunch but we need to get back in the vicinity of Clearwater in twenty."

"Who am I to stand in the way of royalty?"

Nikki grumbled as she peeled off her uniform jacket, then the shirt, then the Kevlar vest.

"Are you really a princess in disguise? Or simply incognito?"

Nikki aimed a mock-scowl at Maura and Seth. "Some silly distant thing between Greece and Denmark that included my great-grandfather's scandalous liaison with a commoner. He was distant royalty, shoved into the armed services for his dalliance and killed in the second world war. But when someone dug up this info and gave it to me, they leaked it to the rest of the sheriff's office." She narrowed her eyes at Maura, and Maura put her hands up in defense.

"Don't look at me."

"And I'm oblivious to most everything," Seth added, and hearing his voice, knowing he stood just a few feet behind her, close enough to touch, made Gianna sigh inside. But then Nikki spoke again, and Gianna swallowed her sigh and put her silly dreams on hold.

"Speaking of your oblivion, Friday night is fine with me. What time do you want to head out?"

"I'm off at two and Tori's home from school by three, so three-thirty?"

"Perfect. That will give us the entire evening, and it doesn't look like we'll be having a significant thaw between now and then."

"Those of us who don't ski hope you're wrong." Maura slipped off her coat as Carmen motioned her over. "Although the romance of a ski lodge isn't lost on me."

Romance? Ski lodge? With the tall, trim and absolutely gorgeous sheriff's deputy?

Turning abruptly, Gianna's rapidly expanding belly nudged a small stack of patterns to the floor. She bent to retrieve them, but Seth beat her to it. "I've got these."

She didn't dare speak, not just yet. Dark emotion swam upward, a combination of Seth in uniform, gorgeous, slim female deputies and her wide girth that allowed little freedom of movement these days.

"When is the baby due?" Nikki asked, but before Gianna could answer, Seth spoke up.

"Babies. Twins. Mid-June, right, Gianna?"

She pressed her mouth into a tight smile and acknowledged the time frame with a quick nod.

"Twins? Really?" Maura laughed as Carmen made short work of measuring her. "That's going to be an adventure."

"You can say that again." Carmen directed a smile at Gianna. "We'll have our hands full, but I expect we'll be surrounded by family come summer and that will lighten the workload."

"Boys? Girls? Did you find out what they are?" A hint of feminine curiosity deepened Nikki's voice.

"One of each."

"How perfect."

Gianna wanted to dislike this woman. Her physical attributes were cover-model friendly. Her gorgeous skin tone made Gianna's more olive complexion seem mottled. And her strong, take-charge attitude left Gianna's questioning nature in the dust. But something about Nikki Peters said they should and could be friends. Except that Nikki was going on a date with Seth on Friday while Gianna sat in the shop running seams and watching the snow fall.

Self-pity snaked up her spine. Time for a change of subject. "How's Tori doing in school, Seth? Is she transitioning well?"

His nod said yes, but his expression marked the situation as "pending." "She loves being back in Kirkwood, but I think she's having a problem fitting in. She missed a lot of school time while she was with her mother."

Gianna's heart ached for the child. She'd been thrust into a situation by no fault of her own and now bore the brunt of the adult decisions surrounding her. "If I can help at all, just let me know. Sometimes kids get less frustrated accepting help from people who aren't their parents." She'd lost her father when she was close to Tori's age, and she understood the difficulties of being different. Conformity ruled the day in junior high. When an entire family suffers a grievous loss, it's hard to support one another. She'd thanked God for Carmen's common-sense advice and love. How would she have gotten through those bitter losses without her grandmother's steady presence?

Your faith. Your beliefs. Your strength comes from the Lord, who made heaven and earth.

She'd sidestepped issues of faith while single in New

York. Sunday work precluded church services, even though bells tolled a welcome each week.

Gianna had ignored the invitation.

And then when she and Michael married, the church service was little more than a nod toward family decorum and a glorious backdrop for pictures.

Something had changed when she'd lost Michael. A stirring of her soul, a quest for meaning beyond the everyday.

She'd hunted for God and found Him, and that growing faith had helped her make the decision to have these babies, to give them their singular chance at life. Right or wrong, she'd quietly taken a side road that would put her mother in a temporary uproar, but eventually—she hoped—Sofia Bianchi Rinaldi would come around.

"Tell her I'd be happy to help with homework or projects. Winter nights are long, and I'm right across the street."

Seth moved slightly, making it impossible to avoid eye contact, and that meant a possible drowning in those baby blues despite the frozen lake outside her door. "I'll tell her. She really enjoyed going shopping with you."

"Gianna's talent for spending money is renowned in our family," Carmen quipped. "And more fun, of course, when it is someone else's funds."

Seth's laugh calmed Gianna's inner turmoil. She was his neighbor, and his tenant. Maybe a new friend.

Funny, you don't sit around and dream about your other friends this way. Kind of telling, isn't it?

She shushed the internal reminder with a cold dose of realism. She'd already lost the two most important men in her life. No way was she about to stand in line to lose another. Friendship and distance were great equalizers.

She made quick work of her measurements and jotted them into the computer that sat to the right of her work area. She scanned the calendar from her seat, then turned back to Nikki. "Can I have you back for a fitting on Friday?"

"That soon? Sure. Is morning okay?"

"Fine." Gianna made a note in the online calendar. "Ten o'clock? We can go earlier or later if you need us to."

"Ten's good. Then I can grab some real food at Tina's place."

"Perfect." Gianna handed her an appointment card with the date and time penciled in. "What made them decide to add women to the undercover force?"

"In my case, I mouthed off to the wrong sergeant," Nikki told her.

Maura laughed. "I did no such thing, and I think the current reasoning is that we can get into places the guys can't. Ladies' rooms, little shops like this. The men would be conspicuous. We'll blend."

Gianna wasn't sure Nikki Peters could ever blend, she was that lovely.

And slim.

"Do they expect trouble at this festival?" Carmen wondered.

"We always expect trouble," Seth admitted. "And then we pray it doesn't come our way. Our proximity to the Canadian border raises awareness. We know that soft targets are becoming more of a lure for terrorism, so it pays to be diligent. When you open the village doors to thousands of tourists for celebratory functions, it's easy for people who mean us harm to slip in." He waved a hand to include the two undercover women. "We want to look like we're part of the scenery but also doing a job. And the local police, deputies and troopers will be out in full measure, so hopefully everything will be fine."

"And your homeland security liaisons?"

Seth faced Carmen directly. "There will be undercover homeland security, yes. But they won't be in costume."

"I think this is a great idea," Carmen said as she finished up with Maura. "You've got the bases covered as best you can. No one can ask for more than that."

Gianna stayed quiet. She wanted more than that. She wanted a written guarantee saying her family, her children, her friends would be safe.

No warranty like that existed, and losing her father, then Michael, reminded her of how quickly life could change.

So that's it? You stop living? You build a bubble and hide in it? Is that how it's going to be? Because I can guarantee you this: toddlers don't like bubbles. The more you protect, the more they struggle for freedom.

She sighed, then caught herself, but not before Seth noticed. But then Seth noticed everything, another reason to stay away from the barrel-chested deputy sheriff. He was too aware, too savvy and way too nice.

He stepped closer to her while Nikki and Maura chatted as they put their coats back on. "You're feeling all right?"

"Fine, thank you."

He hesitated, and that brief moment showed more than she dared see. He leaned in, as if wanting to touch her. Longing to touch her. But then he squared his shoulders, tipped his cap and smiled. "I'm glad to hear it, Gianna."

He moved toward the door, called out a goodbye to Carmen and then swung the door wide briefly for the two women.

He was gone, just like that. She'd had a few minutes of his time, his presence filling a vacuum she tried to ignore, but when he walked into a room, a yearning gaped within her. An emptiness in her heart, begging to be filled.

The uniform put a stop to silly heart-wanderings. And the tall, curvy, gorgeous partner by his side made her see her folly more clearly. Slim-waisted and clear-skinned versus beached whale and blotchy?

She bit back a sigh and stabbed pins into a pattern piece with more velocity than necessary, knowing the answer. And hating it.

CHAPTER NINE

"I CAN COME STRAIGHT HOME TODAY, right, Dad?"

Tori's tone said more than the words, which meant she still didn't like the "wraparound" care he'd signed her up for at the junior high. "Yes."

"You know I'm about the only kid my age that needs a babysitter. It's beyond embarrassing."

Seth acknowledged her comment in typical straightforward fashion. "Yup."

"So why not let me just come home?" Tori crossed the room and stood in front of him, imploring. He didn't dare look down and meet her gaze head-on because he'd cave on the spot. "Think of the money you'll save."

"Money's not a big issue, Tor."

"A penny saved is a penny earned."

"An ounce of prevention is worth a pound of cure," he returned. "Coming home to an empty house day after day is tempting fate. And Grandma's out of our district, so you can't be bussed over there, and she's got Aiden most days, so she can't pick you up."

"I hate it."

He didn't doubt that for a minute. The emotion dripped from her voice and shadowed her face. And it wasn't like he'd had a lot of time to examine options, but he'd have to make it a priority, because seeing her dread school and then dread the after-school program on top of it was driving him crazy. Choices like this hadn't been difficult when she was younger. Back then she was one of the crowd, a shining jewel in the class. Now she was struggling to learn new concepts without a strong basis in middle school education. The principal was keeping an eye on her to see if they should make things easier for Tori by downgrading her back to sixth grade.

She'd cried, hearing that option, and that put him between a rock and a hard place, neither of which made his kid happy.

If he could berate Jasmine for her total lack of sensitivity right now, he would, but that wouldn't do anyone any good, so he handed Tori her insulated lunch bag, grabbed his travel mug and aimed for the door. "Gotta go. And don't think I'm not hearing what you're saying, but I'm working most of the weekend and the first three days of next week. Once that's done I'll check around and see if there's anyone nearby who takes kids after school."

"Another babysitter."

He opened her car door and waited until she dropped into the seat, arms crossed, her face set like a farmyard mule. He leaned in to kiss her cheek, loving her no matter what frustrated expression she sent him. "No. Just a friend to make sure you don't get stolen, killed, attacked or burned up in a fire."

"I'm twelve."

He knew how old she was. But he also understood how easy it was to target latchkey kids, and unsavory characters watched for a chance to find a kid alone. Uh-uh. Not his kid. Not on his watch. He climbed into the driver's seat, put the car in gear and did a K-turn to access the road. "Safety, Tori. That's my main objective, even if I don't win a popularity contest with you. I want you safe. I need you safe." He turned to face her directly before he made the turn onto Lower Lake Road. "I've prayed for you to be safe these past two years, honey. And I expect there were times you weren't."

Her pinched face told him more than he wanted to know, and her little-lost-girl expression broke his heart. "But now you're safe and sound, and if I go a little overboard to keep you that way, it's because I love you." He reached over and hugged her shoulders. "You're my little girl, even if you're not so little anymore."

"I haven't been anyone's little girl in a long time," she whispered, and the way she said the words, as if confessing them, made his chest ache.

"Well, you are now." He kissed her cheek and smiled right into her hazel eyes. "And you're home. So bear with me if I work a little harder than most to keep you protected, okay?"

Her quick nod said she was fighting tears, and seeing her cry filled him with mixed emotions. Was she desperately unhappy? Hormonal? Lonely? Depressed?

Getting to the bottom of her mood swings meant time, but she'd lost so much school time already that he opted for the sensible solution his mother embraced: keep her busy. If Tori was busy enough, she wouldn't have time to feel sorry for herself, or wish she'd been blessed with a normal, loving mother, or lament a past she couldn't change. But as he pulled up in front of the junior high to drop her off, he felt like he was sending her to meet a firing squad. And her face when she turned to wave goodbye?

Said she felt exactly the same way.

"Gianna, would you like some tea?"

Not in this lifetime.

Gianna choked back the words and shook her head. "Nope, I'm good, Gram."

"Well, what about a movie? Would you like a night on the town?"

Kirkwood Lake had one movie theater, halfway around the lake, and it was featuring a you'll-never-sleep-again thriller, which made that a no-go. There were several movie theaters in Clearwater, but Friday nights in the small southern-shore city were filled with high school and college kids. "I'm good, thanks."

"Did Nikki mention what she and Seth were doing tonight?"

Gram had cut straight to the chase, and Gianna worked to keep her face serene. Her grandmother's quirked smile said she hadn't worked hard enough. "I didn't ask but I heard something about a ski lodge."

"The fitting went well on both those girls," Carmen continued. "But I can't pretend it doesn't concern me when the departments go to these lengths to coordinate efforts and plant undercover officers all over a summer festival season."

"I know." Gianna studied the gathered shoulder of Nikki's right sleeve and decided to set it aside rather than shred it. "Is it overkill? Or wizened caution?"

"Caution, I think." Carmen poured boiling water into her ceramic teapot and watched it steep. "But it seems wrong to have to think like that. Every night I thank God for valiant people like Seth and his brother Luke. Nikki and Maura. And Zach, the trooper."

Gianna made a noise of protest as realization dawned. "Oh, Gram. It's your anniversary and I forgot! I'm so sorry. Yes, if you'd like to go out, we still can. It's not too late."

Carmen's face clouded then softened. "No, we don't need to go anywhere. I wasn't really melancholy. It's just hard to see such change. But in the face of danger, it feels good to have a combined police force here that works well together. That's not always the case."

Gianna knew that. Her grandfather's troop had had some rough times with a few local forces in the Adirondack region years ago. By the time she met Michael, law enforcement was less territorial. The terrorist attacks on the World Trade Center and the Pentagon had brought forces together across the nation. "Do you want to play a game? I haven't beaten you at Scrabble in over a week."

Carmen pondered the offer, then shrugged. "I don't think so. I'm going to take my tea into my room and curl up with a book. I'll see you in the morning, darling."

She crossed the room and kissed Gianna's cheek, then disappeared into her first-floor bedroom with her cup, as promised.

Gianna looked around the room and sighed.

Their grand opening wasn't far off now. They were on target for goods and supplies. She'd expended a lot of energy to bring this dream to fruition.

Both dreams, she realized, as one of the twins gave her a swift reminder with a well-placed knee or elbow.

Her own shop. Her own family. Pieces of the past interweaved in a quilt for the future.

The thought gave her peace until she crossed the room to see what Gram had recorded on the DVR. Seth's yard lights shined on the late-day snow across the street. The fresh layer glittered beneath the glow, sparkling like diamond dust. Twin tracks snaked a disappearing path down Seth's driveway, marking his Friday-night date with a beautiful woman.

Not your business.

She repeated the reminder as she used both hands to draw the curtains tightly together, covering the window.

Out of sight, out of mind.

But as she curled into the corner of the comfy sectional to lose herself in mindless TV, images of Seth's Friday-night fun invaded her brain. And that meant TV alone

wouldn't do the trick. TV and freshly made carrot cake?
Maybe.

With a candy bar on the side.

The school bus ground to a stop on Tuesday afternoon
as Gianna stepped outside to survey her window display
from the sidewalk view. The bus paused, the door
squeaked open, then shut before it continued on its path
around the upper lake neighborhoods.

Gianna turned, curious, and saw Tori walking quickly
up the driveway. The cloudless late-February day had
melted any remnants of snow on the asphalt and the sun's
higher path bathed her face with a new warmth, hinting
spring.

Was Seth home?

She didn't think so.

But she also knew that Tori didn't usually come home
on the bus, so why had she taken the bus to an empty
house today?

She knew it wasn't her business. But she also understood
the need within this particular child, as if life had dealt
too many blows.

She went back inside, mulling. Should she cross the
street and check on the girl, or assume everything was
fine? Would she appear nosy and invasive if she walked
over? Or caring and neighborly?

How about lovestruck?

Ridiculous, she fumed as she tugged her heavy sweater
into place. Her coat had refused to button nearly a week
ago, so her heavy sweater had been pressed into service
over layered maternity tops.

Gram was across the docking inlet having coffee with
Tina at the bistro, and if she showed up at Seth's door
looking foolish, well, there would be no one there but
him and Tori to know it. Although that would be bad

enough.

She strode up the driveway and realized that his view came at the cost of a total-body workout to access the house. Either that, or she'd been spending way too much time sitting lately. As she rounded the corner, she stopped, screeched and put a hand to her chest. "Tori, hey! You scared me!"

Red-rimmed eyes, cold hands, a runny nose and tear-streaked cheeks said Tori was in some kind of trouble. Gianna put an arm around the half-frozen girl, lifted the damp backpack that had been sitting on the back step and led the way down the drive, across the street and into the welcoming warmth of the vintage kitchen. "First things first," she ordered as she helped Tori peel off her jacket and hang it near the living room fireplace. "What's wet, what's not and what do you want to eat?"

Tori's face said she'd asked all the right questions. As Gianna set about finding clothing to fit the almost-teenage girl, she thanked God she'd taken the chance to intrude. Whatever had pushed Tori to come home unexpectedly got firmly nudged into second place behind food, clothing and homework. She'd tackle the rest later, once Seth knew what was going on.

"We're losing daylight." Grim, Seth folded his arms as combined rescue teams tried to navigate ice-strewn waters to rescue half a dozen fishermen stranded on a floe that broke free from the western shoreline. "One more pass before it's too dark?"

"If things go perfectly." The fire chief motioned above. "If we don't get them this time, we might not have visibility enough to venture into the water safely until first light." He scowled as the crew reconnoitered. The helicopter buzzed overhead, the loud sound minimizing conversation. The chopper pilot kept the spotlight aimed at the churning waters, but a brisk west wind and the bobbing action of the now-loose ice made centering the light nearly impossible. "The National Weather Service issued warnings about ice fishing today, that the combination of increased sun time and water movement could start breaking up the ice. But nobody listens. Everybody thinks they're invincible."

Seth couldn't disagree. Warnings had been issued and ignored. Ambulances lined the point's main road. Rescue vehicles clogged the entire end of Warrentown. Barricades had been set up to prevent locals from streaming in to see the action because the narrow point couldn't handle a huge influx of vehicles. If they rescued these men, and right now that seemed to be a major "if," they'd need clean streets to rush them to medical care in Clearwater.

He'd texted his mother about picking up Tori and keeping her until he got home. At this moment he had no clue when that might be.

Zach Harrison came up on Seth's right. "Clearwater Fire and Rescue reports one man in the water as of seventeen hundred hours."

The Warrentown fire chief's face went taut. Ice-cold water-induced hypothermia didn't take long to set in. Their time frame had suddenly shrunk to minutes, not hours. As the sun tipped further west, the wind softened. The airboat captain and the helicopter pilot made use of the narrow window of time and daylight to dare getting the stranded fishermen to shore. While they focused on the men still clinging to the mobile ice, another small watercraft aimed for the man in the water.

By the time all was said and done, one man had died and five were taken to the local hospital for treatment. The late hour and frigid darkness grabbed Seth as he traded the squad cruiser for his SUV at the sheriff's office. He hit his Bluetooth connection once his car had defrosted, and called his mother. "Hey, I'm on my way to pick up Tori. Can you have her ready to go? I'm beat."

A short hesitation sent prickles down his back. "I don't have Tori, Seth."

The prickles turned to knife-point awareness. "What do you mean? I texted you this afternoon because Luke and I were on that ice-water rescue. Mom, you're kidding right? And it's not funny, by the way."

"I'm not kidding. I never got your text, and I haven't heard a thing from the Wraparound Care people, and I'm your backup pickup person. Why wouldn't they have called me?" Dismay deepened his mother's voice. "I'm heading to your house now. Maybe she just went home. We know she isn't fond of the after-school program."

Fear didn't sneak up Seth's spine. It claimed him from within, gut-wrenching, mind-numbing fear. Had Jasmine come back and taken Tori from school? Had Tori fallen into some kind of danger, and he had no clue what was wrong because he was unreachable? Why hadn't he gotten her a phone? Why didn't he make sure she could check in as needed?

Regret compounded the fear, but then a call-waiting sound buzzed. "Mom, I'll call you right back. Someone's trying to get ahold of me."

He hit the button for the second call and Gianna's voice came through the phone. "Seth? It's Gianna. I've been trying to reach you but your phone must not be working right. I've got Tori at my place."

"Gianna, you have no idea how happy you just made me. She's been there all the while? She's all right?"

She didn't let him go further. Was that because she sensed the manic fear in his gut? Or did she have the phone on speaker and didn't want the fear in his voice to scare his kid?

More likely.

"She's safe and sound. We tackled math with amazing gusto, and I'm teaching her to pin patterns to fabric.

What's your ETA?"

"Ten minutes. You're sure she's okay?" He wanted to ask more, so much more, but common sense told him to back off. Calm down. Inhale.

"I'm fine, Dad. Gianna's teaching me to sew!" Obviously on speakerphone, and happy, which would have delighted him under other circumstances. Right now? He was tempted to lock her up and throw away the key for months if not years like princesses of old. But first he'd lambaste her for not following directions, then hear what brought her to Gianna's door in the first place, with no message to him, thrusting him into long minutes of hair-raising fear, thinking the worst.

Trust.

The word came to him as the clouds broke overhead, the last full winter moon brightening the ice-strewn lake.

Trust whom, he wondered?

Himself? Clearly he needed work, or his kid would have been equipped to call him, a fact he'd remedy ASAP.

Trust Gianna? A part of him longed to do just that, but lies and secrecy would never be a part of his life again.

Trust Tori? A young girl whose past had been checkered by her mother's poor choices?

Trust God, nimrod. The Father. The Son. The Holy Spirit.

God. The Alpha, the Omega.

His heart calmed. The burning ache in his throat eased.

He loved taking charge. He loved protecting others, but every now and again he needed a reminder that God was with him, "Emmanuel". Trust hadn't come easy to him these past few years. Maybe it should again.

CHAPTER TEN

STRETCHING PAINS WOKE GIANNA IN the middle of the night. She'd called Julia Harrison when they took hold in earnest the previous morning. Julia had reassured her, but right now, when Gianna wanted nothing more than to sleep undisturbed for another two hours, the stretching abdominal muscles wrenched her awake.

She didn't want a bracing cup of stupid anemic tea.

She didn't want to work on cute clothes for skinny people.

And she wasn't a bit hungry. She glared at the clock, hauled in a deep breath, shrugged into ugly sweats and headed for the nursery. One way or another, this room was getting painted, and if she had to wait for Seth to do it, she'd be climbing the walls. Therefore she'd do it herself. She set up the roller on the long-handled attachment, opened the white paint for the ceiling, grabbed the stepladder and began cutting in along the ceiling's edge with the tightly bristled brand-new brush.

A small sound made her pause. Then another one followed. Closer. Much closer.

A shiver traveled up her neck. Tiny goose bumps of awareness blanketed her arms. Just as she decided the house might have become home to unnerving rodents, the sound came again. Firmer. Stronger. From outside.

Her heart beat stronger. Harder. Her breath caught unevenly, because whatever was out there, outside the window, was close.

Too close.

"Gianna."

The familiar voice came from below the window's edge. Recognition made her heart beat irregularly for different reasons than she'd had moments ago.

"Gianna, let me in."

She went downstairs to the kitchen door and cracked it open. "What are you doing out here?" she whispered, and while it was tough to put indignation and censure in a hushed tone, she managed it, because Seth looked half contrite, half amused.

"I saw your lights and wanted to make sure everything was all right. Is it?"

"Get in here. And don't wake Gram."

His smile said her scolding didn't hold much weight, and that was good, because what she really wanted to do was thank him for coming across the road and checking on her. "Who's with Tori?"

"She's sound asleep and the doors are locked. I'm sure she has no clue I'm gone, and she was pretty tired after her escapade today. What are you doing?"

"Painting the nursery."

"At four-fifteen?"

"At three-forty-five, actually. That was the start time. First the ceiling, then the walls. I'm determined to get this done."

"Now?" He followed her through the kitchen and up the stairs to the two-bedroom loft above. "Are you crazy?"

"Some think so, but they're wrong," she retorted. She got back to the room, tested the bristles on her brush to make sure they hadn't gotten tacky while she'd gone downstairs, re-dipped the end and started on her last side of trim. "I couldn't sleep. Stretching pains."

"What are those?"

The word *pain* brought worry to his eyes, and while that reaction made her feel good, the date with Nikki kept her grounded in reality. "Just something we pregos go through, I guess."

He put a hand to her arm, and when she looked down he locked gazes with her. "I'd like a better explanation, please."

His take-charge look warmed her. His protective stance did the same. And when she hesitated, he reached up, nipped her around the vicinity of where her waist used to be, and brought her down from the ladder. He took the brush from her, moved up the two steps and started cutting in for her. "Talk. And don't wake Grandma."

His use of her words made her smile. And while she liked his offer of help, she'd come to Kirkwood determined to stand on her own without the influx of lovable but intrusive Italian family members trying to run her life. She'd made the move to declare her independence, which meant she wasn't about to let Seth boss her around, either. Still, it was a fair question. "Abdominal muscles have to stretch to accommodate babies. When they get to a certain point, the stretching becomes painful."

"You're in pain?" The look he aimed at her said he was one step from calling the hospital.

"Just muscle pain. Not labor pains."

"How can you tell the difference?"

Well, there was the question of the hour. "I couldn't, so I called the doctor when they started yesterday. I didn't want to worry Grandma so I didn't say anything, but Julia told me these are normal for this stage of pregnancy, that they usually last a week or two, and then abate."

"What if she's wrong?"

"Why would she be wrong?" That possibility hadn't even occurred to Gianna because Julia had sounded so certain. "She's trained in all this. I'm not. Let's just trust her judgment, okay?"

He didn't look convinced, but he turned back to painting, muttering as he went.

"And stop grumbling. If you don't want to paint get off the ladder and give me back my brush. You're being silly. I'm not sick, I'm pregnant."

"Gianna? Are you awake, dear?"

They'd awakened Carmen.

Irked, Gianna clapped a hand over her mouth. Seth's eyes laughed down at her and he waggled a finger in her direction. "Your fault. I was whispering."

"I'm working in the nursery, Gram. Couldn't sleep. And, um…" She half choked on this admission, wondering what her grandmother's response would be. "Seth's helping, too."

"Good! I was hoping he'd come by soon. I'll make coffee."

Seth's laugh nearly got him smacked. Her grandmother's acceptance of the situation, as if it was perfectly normal to have a neighbor helping before 5:00 a.m., made the moment more ludicrous. "Don't you have to work today?"

"Later. And I have to get back to my house by six for Tori to get up and get to school by seven-fifteen, but this is a pretty nice way to start the day, Gianna. And when Gram gets that coffee done, it will be better yet."

He finished cutting in, then rolled the full ceiling before grabbing his coat to head back across the street nearly an hour later. Carmen had made coffee, then settled herself in the sewing area of the store beyond. The soft hum of her machine said she'd jumped right into some kind of unfinished business. "Don't do the rest," Seth instructed

Gianna as he shrugged into his Carhartt jacket. "I'll come by tomorrow and finish. And if it needs two coats, I'll do the second one on Thursday, because I'm off both days."

"I can do it."

"I know that." He turned and faced her, then cupped her shoulders with two big, broad hands. "But you don't need to. Sit and sew."

Buried emotions spiked within her, a tempest she hadn't known existed until it burst forth. Proximity alone made Seth the target. Well, that and the fact that he'd gone out on a date with a stick-thin beauty a few nights before. "I'm sick of sitting, I'm tired of sewing and I feel like I've been waiting for something to happen… anything to happen! For months. And I'm about to go stark raving mad."

He contemplated her as if weighing her words, her stance, her little tirade, then in one sweeping move he pulled her into his arms, lowered his head and kissed her.

Heart-stopping. Amazing. Delightful. Embracing and loving, the kiss rocked her world into a high gear she thought she'd forgotten years ago.

Wrong.

She hadn't forgotten at all as her heart yearned to be cherished again.

She should end the kiss. Pull back. Step away.

She didn't. She kissed him back, her hands wrapped around his head, the nape of buzzed neck hair bristling against her fingers.

He ended the kiss, scowled at the clock, then moved out the door. "Tori's got to get up. Although in truth, I'd like nothing better than to hang out here awhile longer."

His boyish grin said he'd enjoyed the kiss as much as she had and hadn't wanted it to end.

Ditto.

But as nice as the kiss was, a relationship with Seth was

off-the-radar impossible. She wasn't protecting just her own feelings anymore. She needed to stand guard for the babies' emotions, as well.

Most cops live well beyond retirement age enjoying long, happy, healthy lives. Carmen reminded her of that on a regular basis.

Statistics supported Carmen's advice. But her father and Michael were both gone, and that reality marked her. If once burned was twice careful, what was twice burned? Bordering on three strikes and you're out?

She made a face at Seth, and his eyes said he interpreted the look. But then he reached out a hand and traced one finger along her hair…then her chin…and paused there. "I'll see you tomorrow. Okay?"

"To paint."

He acknowledged that with a tiny, amused quirk to his jaw. "To paint. And we'll have Tori come by after school. I'm sure she'd love to help."

"Tori, yes." Gianna nodded, glad to jump to a different subject that didn't include longing looks and sweet goodbye kisses. "I wanted to ask you, but not with her around." She stepped closer. Seth leaned the door closed while she talked, shutting the cold stream of late-winter air out. "Can she come here after school instead of the school program she was attending?"

"Well, I—" His expression said she'd surprised him, and she didn't think too much surprised a cop like Seth Campbell.

"She liked it here," Gianna continued. "And we enjoyed having her around."

"It was nice having a youngster in the house, Seth!" Carmen's voice called out from the shop beyond the curtain. "And she wants to learn to sew. And Gianna is very good at math."

"I expect she's good at a great many things," Seth called back, and his tone revealed nothing.

The knowing look he shot to Gianna said he'd just discovered another hidden talent.

She blushed.

He grinned.

"Oh, she is!" Carmen called back. Her machine clicked back into gear and Seth softened the volume of his voice to talk with Gianna.

"Do you really want a kid hanging around here?"

"Absolutely. And she hates going to the wraparound care so why put her through that?"

"Because I was between a rock and a hard place with little recourse."

"Which we've just changed," Gianna argued. "So let her come here, and she and I can address her math skills while I teach her to appreciate a bias seam and opera."

"If it makes my kid happy, I can deal with whatever the seam thing is." He paused as if struggling, then pretended to acquiesce with a hiked brow. "But opera, Gianna? Really? Do we have to go that far?"

"I'll have her belting with The Three Tenors by the end of the week."

Seth pushed through the storm door and strode down the driveway, but the sound of his laughter stayed with Gianna long after he'd disappeared into his house.

Seth.

Tori.

The kiss.

Are you trying to complicate your life further? Because you know it's a given if you follow this path. A path to nowhere, by the way.

Gianna shushed the internal scolding and went upstairs. The scent of fresh paint wafted out of the nursery. Her babies' room, soon to be occupied by two tiny lives. Did she dare move forward with Seth? See where this attraction would lead? Did she have courage enough? Strength enough? Faith enough?

Isaiah preached of God's great love in a time of want and need. Gianna looked at the sweet room, almost ready to be filled with furniture. Her simple, shabby-chic room across the upstairs sitting area. Soft carpet beneath her feet. Food in the cupboards. Warmth and shelter from the storm.

She had so much. Despite her losses, God had blessed her with comfort and family who loved her. Maybe it was time to get over anger at what she couldn't control and show a little more gratitude for what she'd been gifted.

One of the babies churned inside her. The other responded in kind, already duking it out for space and her attention.

A thin streak of light hit the underside of the overhead cloud front, and the combination of the near sunrise and the clouds produced a wave of bright colors. Greens, yellows, tangerines and a hint of pink spread forth.

The colors would disappear as the sun's arc tipped behind the low pressure system dogging the Great Lakes, but at this moment the horizon held celestial beauty, a brightness she longed to carry in her heart forever.

Then do it. Move forward. You've already made big decisions. Keep going.

She would. No matter what happened with Seth, meeting him…knowing him…yes, kissing him…made her realize she still had a future. Better to let God lay those paths before her than erect more roadblocks, because the truth was she'd loved working on this room with Seth.

And she wouldn't mind another kiss. Or two.

CHAPTER ELEVEN

A S SETH STEPPED INTO THE unscheduled meeting called by the mixed group of law enforcement commanders, one person stood out from the rest.

Tall. Broad-shouldered. Tough gaze. And a tattoo that traveled from somewhere beneath his collar up to his neck. He wore some kind of name tag clipped to a low-profile brown serge jacket and carried a roll of papers under his left arm as if guarding them. The room reeked of trouble, and the expressions on the various commanders' faces said likewise.

Seth's boss, Sheriff Drew Jackson, stepped up to the podium, looking none too pleased. "We have a misstep in our bicentennial planning."

A misstep?

Seth caught Zach Harrison's eye across the room. They'd been coordinating the combined efforts of the various forces for nearly a year to make sure things would run smoothly during the coming tourist season. They'd checked and rechecked everything, with their commanders on board. What had they done wrong?

"It seems the state of New York neglected to inform us of some timely information."

The man with the tube of papers didn't move a muscle. He stood there, with over thirty gazes trained on him, and the guy took it.

His non-reaction moved him up a step in Seth's opinion.

"The state-wide bridge project has decided to choose this year—our bicentennial year—" the sheriff drew out the word *bicentennial* to make a valid point about bad timing "—to close roads. I'm going to turn you over to Rye Gallagher to explain how this came about."

The man stepped forward. He didn't look apologetic, he didn't look defensive. Nothing about him said combative, but the way he moved to the microphone in a room full of armed officers said little provoked this guy because he was in complete control of a given situation. And that hiked Seth's appraisal higher yet.

He faced the commanders, and his first words set the stage. "Six people died in a bridge collapse downstate four years ago. Three people lost their lives when a creek bridge was swept downstream in the Adirondacks. And last fall's flooding of Kirkwood Lake's southern basin undermined two local bridges, putting them at critical risk." He tapped a remote control and a large screen behind him lit up. "The bridge leading from Old Water Road to Upper Lake Road will have to be closed. The bridge from Lower Lake Road to Log Cabin Road will also have to be closed, which means traffic will have to be detoured across the interstate."

Across the interstate meant that people who wanted to circle the lake for the various points of interest and festivals would have to drive many miles out of their way during their busiest tourist season.

Seth and Zach exchanged glances. Nikki and Maura moved closer to Seth's side. "Of all the stupid, lamebrained, last minute—"

The bridge guy's gaze zeroed in on Nikki. He stood there, silent and square-shouldered, then hiked one brow. "Did you have a question, officer?"

"Deputy," she shot back. "It's nearly March. When were

you expecting to let us know? When the barricades went up? It didn't occur to the suits in Albany that we might actually have lives to live on this side of the state? Because this goes beyond inconvenient. You've pretty much put a death sentence on half of the bicentennial functions."

"I think this meeting answers that question, Deputy." He answered her with a calm demeanor, but something in his stature said he understood her question and her anger, even if he didn't necessarily like her methods. "The state ordered the immediate closure as of seventeen-hundred hours yesterday. I drove straight here because my investigation showed this was a rough time to be making these choices, but that decision is out of my hands. Making the bridge safe again?" He swept the room an honest look. "That's my job. And we're researching some temporary alternatives on at least one of the bridges, but it might take a few days before I can assess their feasibility."

Nikki bristled alongside Seth. Maura put out a restraining hand, reminding Nikki to think before she spoke. For once it worked, and Seth breathed a little easier, right until Drew spoke again. "Seth, Zach, Nikki and Maura. Can I put you four on a committee with Mr. Gallagher to come up with an alternative plan?"

Seth hadn't become a decorated deputy by refusing commands. "Of course, sir."

"Certainly. Is tonight convenient?" Zach asked.

"Yes." Gallagher flicked off the PowerPoint screen. "I'm staying at the Comfort Inn in Clearwater, so we could meet in their first-floor conference room. Four o'clock?"

Four o'clock meant Seth would be calling Gianna to see if she could keep Tori longer. If she couldn't, his parents would be free to pick up Tori by then. Seth nodded as some of the gathered officers moved toward the door, ready for the shift change. "Sure."

"We'll be there." Maura answered for her and Nikki, then rolled her eyes at Seth. "The two hours will give

Nikki time to calm down," she whispered, but made sure Nikki would hear. "With enough caffeine in her system to keep her from getting snippy."

Nikki scowled, then sighed. She faced the window for a long, drawn-out moment, then turned back to Seth and Maura. "I'm fine. And I won't shoot the messenger. This guy's just an underling doing the bidding of morons at the top, so I'll cut him some slack."

"Nice of you, Deputy."

Nikki froze in place.

Maura looked like she wanted the floor to drop open and swallow them whole.

Seth met Gallagher's gaze and indicated the clock on the wall above the door. "We'll be there at four, Mr. Gallagher."

"Rye." He leaned in and extended a hand to Seth. "Thank you, Deputy."

He moved out the door with a lumbering roll to his shoulders and his gait, and Seth was pretty sure if a bridge required it, this guy could probably hold up one end on his own, Atlas-style.

"Shoot me now." Nikki stared after the bridge engineer, dismayed. "When will I learn to just shut up? Smile and nod? Say 'Yes, sir' and mean it?"

"Soon," Seth suggested as the sheriff sent Nikki a look of unmasked displeasure. "Let's hope it's soon."

"Tori? Your dad's here." Carmen bustled into the living room. Seth followed her, but when he opened his mouth to apologize for the late hour, Gianna silenced him with one hand up.

"Shush, it's fine. We've got something to show you. Come over here."

"Two things, Dad!" Clearly pleased with herself, Tori pointed to the laptop screen. "Check out this test score."

"Ninety-eight percent?" He leaned closer and saw that the test covered multiple properties of sixth-grade math. "Tori, that's wonderful."

"Gianna found this site, and it moves you along as fast as it thinks you can go. We started on some really lame fifth-grade stuff around three o'clock and—"

"And we haven't left the site for more than a quick bite of supper, and by quick I mean she inhaled her food," Gianna told him as Tori's grin widened. "And a bathroom break. So tomorrow she can move to the next sixth grade unit. If she barrels through these online lessons the way I think she will, she'll be up to grade level by the end of the year. Or before."

"Definitely before," Tori told them. She stood, stretched and yawned, then hugged Seth quickly. "I never knew it was so easy to find things like this online. And Gianna knows everything about math and science."

"Well." Gianna pretended humility with a teasing face and an exaggerated shrug. "I don't like to brag, but math and science were my forte. I went to Rutgers determined to be a biochemist and discover cures for grave illnesses, thereby saving the world."

"What happened?" Tori stared up at her, wondering. "Did you drop out?"

Gianna shook her head. "Nope. I took a couple of costume design electives in their school of the arts and—"

"Sewing won your heart."

Seth's easy summation was spot-on. Gianna sent her grandmother a look of shared empathy. "I love the creative side of fabric. The be-my-own-boss inventiveness. And while I was in college I got a chance to intern in New York, on Broadway. By my sophomore year, I'd realized what I wanted to do. So I did it."

Tori hugged her impulsively. "I'm glad you did," she whispered. "It's important to follow your dreams, right?"

One of the babies took aim at Tori's right arm, and the girl stepped back, laughing. "I got kicked!"

"It's like housing Rock'em Sock'em Robots these days," Gianna replied. Then she took Tori's left hand and placed it on her rounded belly. "Leave your hand here for just a minute."

Tori's eyes grew round a few seconds later. "Something's nudging me."

"Yup. Bony, right?"

"Yes."

Seth's face said he wanted to feel the baby move, too, but didn't dare ask. Gianna reached out, took his hand and placed it just above Tori's. Then she waited until his eyes went round. "I think he high-fived me."

"The boy, huh? It couldn't have been the girl?"

He slanted a very serious look down to her. "It was a distinctly manly high five."

She laughed as Tori moved back. "Does it hurt when they kick?"

"Not really. More like feels odd." She made a face that said explaining it was hard. "But it's getting crowded in there." Gianna settled her hand at the top of her curved belly. "And we've got over three months to go, so it will be interesting. Right now they think they've got room to move. My body is not in full agreement with their theory."

Seth's phone buzzed. He picked it up, glanced at the readout and let the call go to voice mail.

"Not important?" Tori asked as she tugged on her jacket and grabbed her backpack.

"Nikki. We were caught up in a meeting tonight, and I'm sure she wants to touch base on a few things. Nothing that can't wait."

A date with Nikki. Working with Nikki. A meeting that held him late at work with Nikki.

Gianna had a trusting nature, but she wasn't born

yesterday, and she had no intention of being caught in the middle of some small-town police triangle of dating one woman while kissing another one senseless. Not gonna happen.

"Gianna, thank you!" Tori hugged her again, eyes shining. "And thank you for letting me come over here to hang out and work. It was so much fun!"

"I'm glad." She put a gentle kiss on the girl's cheek and swung the door wide. "I'll see you tomorrow, okay?"

"Yes. Bye!"

"And I'll be over to finish the room once Tori's on the bus," Seth promised as he turned to follow Tori out the door. "Thank you, Gianna."

"No problem, but I can do the room myself, Seth. In fact, I'd rather do it myself. You understand, I'm sure."

He turned her way, puzzled, and he studied her face in that cop way that made her crazy wondering what cops saw or thought they saw. Tori yelled for him because he had the house key. He paused, clenched his jaw, waved to Carmen and repeated himself. "I'll be here by seven-thirty. Coffee would be nice."

He turned and strode up her driveway to road level, then angled his way to his place across the road.

Carmen came up next to Gianna and reached out to shut the door. "It's getting cold," she explained. "I'm heading off to bed, dear. I'll see you in the morning."

"It's early," Gianna protested, but Carmen waved a hand.

"My day started earlier than usual today. As did yours," her grandmother added as she slipped into her room.

It had. Funny, she hadn't felt a bit overtired with Tori here. Or when Seth had strolled in to pick up his daughter. But now a different weariness grabbed hold of her, based on ornery, jealous emotions that should have no place in her life or her heart.

She turned out the lights and dragged an overstuffed

recliner to the living room window overlooking the lake. Another clear night, still wicked cold, but the higher sun had shifted and melted more ice today. The moonlight draped a path across the elongated body of water, and the swath of light danced with the movement of ice and wind.

She sat there, watching the ice bob until her eyes grew tired. Stretched out in the recliner, sleep claimed her as she worked to put thoughts of Seth and Nikki out of mind. Just before she dozed off, her phone vibrated an incoming text. The sound jerked her awake, but the text—and the sender—made it much easier to fall asleep once she'd read the message.

Nikki is a friend and a cop. We work together. You're being silly. And btw, I've never kissed Nikki Peters, but I can't stop thinking about kissing Gianna Costanza again. Soon, I hope. Sleep well.

He'd read her like an open book. And it felt good. More than good, it felt wonderful, like a quiet kiss good-night.

She tucked the phone on the table next to the big easy chair and dozed off, peaceful.

"The room looks great, Seth. Thank you."

He finished scrubbing dots of yellow from his fingers and glanced over his shoulder as he dried his hands. "You're welcome. Stay off ladders. If you want something done requiring a ladder, ask me. I'll take care of it."

"I'm not big on asking for help."

"I get that." He rehung the towel, rolled his shoulders to ease the stiffness and then made himself another cup of coffee from their brewing system. "But if you're willing to help me with Tori and that whole after-school fiasco, why can't I expect the same in return?"

"I hate sensible men."

He laughed, and his expression said he didn't believe her. "There's nothing wrong with independence. But insisting on doing everything yourself can be self-defeating. Isn't that why we live in communities? To support one another?"

"You have never been raised—wait, let's change that to *smothered*—by a big, fun, intrusive Italian family."

"They can't be that bad." Seth's doubtful look deepened. "Family's family."

Carmen laughed out loud from the living room and came into the kitchen. She shook a finger at Seth as she pulled on her wool tweed jacket. "You are wrong, but you will see the error of your ways when they arrive en masse. And you'll understand that while I love my family, they are worse than a bunch of clucking hens when things happen. Everyone with an opinion and running from house to house, talking, yapping."

She pulled on the bright red scarf that had become her signature around town and leaned down to kiss Gianna's cheek. "I'm going to Tina's to have my afternoon tea. She and I like to talk about things, and I think I might just ask her about a certain Campbell boy named Max."

Seth grimaced. "Watch your step. Max is one-of-a-kind and a sore subject with Tina, I expect."

"I'm not so sure that's true." Carmen smiled at him. "Brave, strong, true, honest, ambitious. I'd say it's a family trait."

"Thanks, Carmen."

She swung open the kitchen door and breathed deep, delighted. "Do you smell that?"

"What?" Gianna turned, puzzled.

"Spring. I smell spring."

The March day had warmed considerably while they painted inside. The clear blue sky had lost the thin shade of winter, and the sun shone with a strength they hadn't felt in long, dark months.

"I'll leave the door open," Carmen said as she left. "Let some fresh air in."

"It feels good." Gianna stood in a sunbeam and stretched, catlike. "Like you could soak it into your bones."

"So when are they due back?"

Gianna winced inside. She was pretty sure he'd get back on topic, but she was less sure how much she wanted to say. Or not say. "My family?"

He didn't answer because of course that was what he meant. She poured a glass of water and sat down at the kitchen table opposite him. "The end of April."

"That's a long time yet."

She didn't really need help with the math, so she nodded, waiting.

"Which means living a lie for almost two more months."

She'd eyed the calendar that very morning, wondering why she was waiting this long. What would her mother say? How hurt would she be that her only daughter didn't trust her enough to be honest with her? And how upset would she be with Carmen, her mother?

Mother and daughter were cut from a different cloth, but they loved each other. Keeping her mother out of this early on had made some sense because Gianna knew she couldn't handle the weight of countless opinions, half of which would think she was crazy and would doubt her ability to handle things. She'd already proven that wrong.

But now? What was the sense now?

"You're afraid to own up."

She stared out the window, then put her head in her hands. "Putting off the inevitable, I guess."

"Man up, Costanza."

He didn't sympathize, didn't cajole. He challenged her, and she liked that about him. "I have to, don't I?"

He flexed his upper arm again and she stood up, rounded the table and put her hands on his shoulders. "Hold still. I'll rub that sting out for you."

"I won't refuse. I messed up that shoulder playing football back in the day and when I overextend it reminds me. Nothing major. Just—" He stopped talking as she kneaded the muscle beneath her hands, and then he sighed, chin down. "That's beyond wonderful."

She laughed. "Good. It's the least I can do for you. I love how the room looks, so bright and cheerful. And I know when my family returns, they're going to want to throw a shower for me, so I don't have much to put in the nursery yet, but it's nice to know it's ready."

"I think Piper picked the exact same color," Seth told her. "Zach had a spot of it on his wrist the other day. I was so jealous when I heard they were expecting. Happy for them, but jealous because Tori was gone and I had no way of contacting her. Seeing her. Making sure she was okay. And now?" He leaned back, stretched, and his more relaxed smile said his shoulder felt better. "I feel blessed beyond words. She's here, and yeah, she's got issues, but I can deal with those, step-by-step. It was the not knowing that was killing me." He sent her a look that said more. Much more.

"You want me to tell my family." Which meant telling Michael's mother, as well.

He stood, grabbed his Carhartt jacket and didn't hesitate. "I think you *want* to tell them. It's the honest thing to do, and you don't want your grand opening overshadowed by your conscience. So get going."

He was correct. She was making things worse by waffling. She pointed to the door. "Go home. I can't make a phone call like this with anyone around."

He didn't kiss her, or hug her. Instead he cupped her shoulders in those two big hands and gently bumped foreheads with her, a total guy thing. "When our women fail in courage, shall our men be fearless still?"

"You read *Anne of Green Gables*? Why do I find that odd?"

He laughed and chucked her on the chin. "Didn't read it, but my sister Addie had that on her wall growing up. My parents adopted her when she was almost five years old, and she said later it was like coming home to her very own Green Gables. Except with a lot of smelly boys."

She liked his family, the few she'd met. And from the sound of it, she'd like Addie. For now, she needed to bite the bullet. Call her mother.

She didn't hesitate once Seth had walked out the door. She grabbed her phone, hit the number two on her speed-dial, and when her mother answered, she drew a deep breath and waded in. "Mom? It's Gianna. I've got something to tell you...."

CHAPTER TWELVE

SETH DREW HIS JACKET COLLAR tighter as he headed to his SUV after work the next afternoon. A low-pressure system had pushed in from the upper Great Lakes, bringing rain and sleet to the Northeast. Strong winds accompanied the system, and he wished he'd gotten new gutters on the far side of the house, because this storm was going to put the old ones to the test.

As he headed for the Interstate exit leading to the north end of the lake, his phone buzzed. Tina's number flashed on his dashboard. He hit the connect button. "Tina, what's up? Do you need something?"

Every now and again she'd have him grab supplies from Clearwater. Running a restaurant independently didn't leave her a lot of shopping time, and if she ran low on something he'd swing by the wholesale club in Clearwater for her.

"Jasmine's here."

He'd been waiting to hear those words since Tori returned. He thought he was ready to see his ex-wife, face her and deal with the battle that was sure to come. On top of that her presence would bring more mixed emotions to a nearly teenage girl who had never been first in her mother's life.

Anger gripped him deep within. Fear met the anger head-on and wrestled for control. Had she come to take Tori back? Was she here to grab the kid and run, or was she waiting to see what he'd offer in exchange for making him Tori's guardian? And had he put aside enough money to cut the deal?

"Where is she?"

"She was in here, looking for you. And looking for Tori. I played dumb."

"Thank you, Tina."

"Well, she's not happy with me, and I can't say I went overboard being nice, but I was straight with her. Said you'd be home around six. But I didn't want you blindsided."

"Tori's at Gianna's. I'll call over there and tell them to lay low for a while. Unless she saw Tori get off the bus." Did Jasmine know her daughter was three hundred feet up the road? Gianna's grand opening was three days away, and he'd promised Tori she could help the ladies on the weekend. She'd been delighted by the prospect of working with Gianna and Carmen in a real store.

Jasmine's unexpected arrival might change that and a whole lot more, but he'd suspected this would happen so now he needed to act. Usually it was a task he did well. Today, with Jasmine's casual treatment of God's precious gift, a child? He wasn't sure he could stay calm, cool and collected.

He pulled around the back of his house, parked and faced the road as an aged Chevy pulled up the driveway behind him. He stood ramrod-straight and tall, wondering what to say and what not to say, praying he wouldn't push Jasmine over some fine line.

Her car door groaned, begging for a shot of WD-40 as she shoved it open. She climbed out of the driver's seat and Seth was unprepared for what he saw. The woman before him was a faint imitation of the woman he'd married ten years before. Dark circles rimmed what used to be vibrant green eyes. Dull hair showed a combination of neglect and lack of nutrients. Her color looked sallow, and her prominent cheekbones aged her well beyond her thirty-two years.

She didn't look healthy or happy, but he noted a difference as she walked his way: She looked calm.

He was ready for a fight, if needed. Or at least a bargaining session, where she made demands and he countered with what he could afford, but her first words surprised him and hiked his faith in human nature. "I've got the guardianship papers you'll need." She handed him an envelope as she continued. "They're all signed and notarized, just like you asked."

"And?" Seth found himself at a loss for words. What did she want in return? What was she after? And how long would she be in town?

"And that's it." She breathed out and watched the encroaching cold night turn her breath into vapor. "I shouldn't have taken her with me. And I never should have let things go on as long as they did, but she's here now. Where she belongs. That's what matters, right?"

He longed to berate her, because whatever indignities Tori had suffered would have been avoided if she'd just left the girl with him.

Isaiah's words flooded his heart and soul. "Can a mother forget the baby at her breast and have no compassion for the child she has borne? Though she may forget, I will never forget you."

Consideration helped choose Seth's next words. "If you need help, why don't you stay here, Jasmine? Whatever's gone wrong, there are people and places that can help you."

She gave a harsh laugh and lit a cigarette with shaking hands, and that moment of flickering light underscored the gravity of her choices. "That's not going to happen. I don't belong here, Seth. I never did. But that wasn't your fault." She puffed out a cloud of smoke then turned to contemplate him and the house behind him. "I wanted to be happy. I wanted to be picket-fence normal, but I hated it. Not you." She turned and shrugged a shoulder in his direction. When she did, the loose jacket slipped down and he made out the thinness of her frame.

Realization struck him. She was sick. Maybe seriously. As he moved forward, she jumped, startled, a deer-in-the-headlights look holding him at bay. "You're not well. Stay here, in town. We'll get you some medical help, we'll—"

"You don't get it do you?" Old anger hardened her gaze. "I'm not meant for here. Never was. But when I was a kid I read this story about a woman in England. She lived in the country, and there was this cat that came to get warm by the fire. Didn't stay long and the cat was no one's friend, but now and again she'd come, nip a bite to eat and warm herself. One day the cat came in as usual, and in her mouth she carried a little kitten. She laid the kitten on the rug and left. She never came back, but the old woman knew why she'd brought the little cat inside to the fire. Because the old cat wanted more for her child than she had for herself."

She coughed hard, took another drag on the cigarette, then ground out the butt. "The shrinks say it's not good for a mother to abandon her child. I expect you to help her with that, Seth. Make it seem not so bad. Because we both know in this case it's the best choice for all concerned."

Remorse warred with caution inside him. Should he insist she stay? Push her to get help? "Jasmine, stay here. Just until you're strong enough to move on. It's—"

"I'll write when I can. Just to let her know I haven't forgotten her. And that in my own way, I really did love her." She climbed back into the car and Seth moved forward.

"I've got money, Jasmine. Let me—"

"I won't, but I appreciate the offer. Tell her to expect

a letter now and again. And tell her…" she didn't face him to say these next words, and he read the emotional struggle in her face and neck. She clenched her jaw, pulled in a quick breath and pushed out the words. "I'm sorry. So dreadfully sorry. I want her to have a good life."

"I will. I promise. I—"

She backed down the driveway slowly, not hearing his promise. But then she knew him well. Unlike her, he always kept his word.

As the car rumbled off into the night, he scrambled to get the license plate number. He committed it to memory, then went inside to examine the papers she'd given him. All in order, exactly as he'd requested before she'd run off. Tucked into the corner of the envelope was a tiny plastic resealable bag. Inside the bag was the ring he'd given Jasmine for their engagement. A scrap of paper with Tori's name scrawled on it was folded inside the bag. And behind the sheaf of papers was a newborn-sized outfit, a white background covered with pink rosebuds, gently folded and tucked in the corner of the envelope.

Where had she kept this tiny outfit for so many years?

Seth had no idea, but this single manila envelope held hints of Tori's past and a promise for her future. He took a deep breath, tucked the envelope into his safe and headed across the street to pick up his beautiful daughter. Legally she might be called his "ward," but emotionally?

She was his, and the thought of having the legal hassles behind him calmed heart rhythms that had been out of sync for two long years.

But not anymore.

He knocked on Gianna's door, and when Tori answered it, he grabbed her into a hug.

"Dad. You okay?"

"I'm fine." He grinned down at her, relieved beyond words. Yes, he'd have to tread softly about the issue of her mother. But he could do it at his own pace, putting prayer and thought behind it. Because once and for all, this beautiful child was his and he couldn't be happier.

"Her mother was here?" Gianna faced Seth as Carmen walked Tori across the road a few minutes later. "Tonight?"

"Yes, and for all the right reasons." Seth's gaze followed Carmen and Tori's progress as he spoke. "She left me signed guardianship papers and a couple of mementos for Tori."

"Will she stay?" Gianna paced the small kitchen as she considered the ramifications. "Because if she does, we can—"

"She's gone. And I don't think she'll be coming back, Gianna."

"No?" She turned, read his expression and took a seat. The grim note in Seth's tone matched the set of his jaw. "How bad is she, Seth?"

"Illness. Addiction. Emotional instability." He ticked off his fingers as he went down the list, then stopped and sat down next to her. "But I'm thanking God she did the right thing by bringing Tori here. That no matter what happened, she put Tori first. She's never done that before."

"Desperation makes a tough mirror," Gianna told him.

He contemplated her words as he took her hand. "I didn't know what to say, but it turns out I didn't have to say anything. For over two years I've been mentally rehearsing how to win Tori back from her mother, and in the end, it was answered prayer. And a story about a cat."

A cat? Gianna gave him a blank look. "You lost me."

"She told me about this story she read when she was a little kid, about a cat who comes to visit an old lady, then brings the lady a kitten."

"Wait here." Gianna went upstairs to the pile of boxes sitting outside the freshly painted nursery. She opened one, rummaged through a small stack, grabbed what she was looking for and hurried back downstairs. "This is it. The story she was telling you about."

"The Christmas Day Kitten." Seth frowned. "I've never seen this before."

"Gram is a big James Herriot fan, and she always loved this story. When they came out with a children's edition, she bought it for me. The story is about the mother cat's sacrificial love, how her last act is to save the life of her child. I've probably read it a hundred times over the years."

"And you brought it with you to read to the twins."

She inhaled deeply, then tapped the book lightly. "When Michael and I got married, we had so many plans. We were both goal-oriented, focused and driven, so we never imagined things wouldn't go our way. Up until that point, we'd both gotten exactly what we wanted out of life. When we couldn't conceive we decided to use in vitro help at the fertility clinic near Albany. If God couldn't give us a baby, science would."

She faced him square and went on. "That was pretty much my attitude back then. If something didn't go my way, I worked long and hard to make it happen."

"That's not a bad attribute, Gianna."

"When controlled, no. But it's kind of like ambition, Seth. A good servant, but a bad master. Anyway, I got pregnant, then miscarried and I was mad. So mad. Mad at myself, mad at my body, mad at everything, because how come I was the one thwarted? All around me friends and family were having babies, making playdates, growing fat and round with pregnancy, and I couldn't make it work."

He laid his hand over hers but stayed gently quiet.

"We tried again with two of our frozen embryos. Once again I got pregnant, but we'd learned a hard lesson. We didn't dare hope. Didn't dare dream. But about eight weeks along we started to believe that maybe, just maybe, things would work out." She sighed deeply and stared at the big, broad hand covering hers. A deputy's hand. A man in uniform, pledged to serve and save. "I wanted ice cream and we didn't have any. And all the stores were closed by us, but there was a little convenience store a few miles away that stayed open late. Michael got dressed, went to the store, and when he got there, he interrupted a robbery in progress. He didn't even have time to pull his weapon. The guy panicked, turned and shot. Mike wasn't wearing his vest, and he probably walked into that store thinking about me. About the baby. And then he was gone. Just gone."

"Gianna." Seth's hand gripped hers. He held tight as if wanting to help, but it was an old story now, though the retelling always choked her with emotion.

"I lost the baby a few weeks later. Despite all my plans, my hopes, my very organized dreams, I was left with nothing. No husband, no baby, and for a little while—" she paused, made a face, then admitted "—a long while, I didn't care about anything. I was a shell, existing. A fairly crazy shell, if you must know."

"Your family must have been worried sick."

She sent him a watery smile and dashed tears aside with her free hand. "Well, when you meet them you'll understand. They mean well, and I was overly sensitive, but they're not a bit discreet and crazy dramatic to boot. So they were pretty sure I was going crazy, too."

"But you didn't go crazy."

"I found faith." She said the words softly, letting the peace of going outside herself and her needs bathe her. "In all that void there seemed to be only one thing that helped. Talking to God. Once I quit yelling at Him, of course."

"I did my share of that. I get it."

She squeezed his hand. "Every year I received a storage bill from the fertility clinic. We had two embryos still in cold storage. And last spring, when I got the bill, I started thinking and praying. These two babies had done nothing wrong. They didn't ask to be conceived. They didn't come into being accidentally. We had planned to make a host of embryos to complete our family, but all of a sudden I saw what we'd done. We'd created life as if it was a scientific convenience, not a soul-stirring creation. I prayed. I thought. And I talked to Gram." She shrugged. "And then I quietly went through the treatments to get pregnant, even though I knew the odds of carrying the pregnancy were tenuous with my track record. If I didn't at least try, these babies had no chance at all. And that didn't seem fair."

"Maternal love and sacrifice." Seth reached over and hugged her, and the hug felt good. So good. "Gianna, you're a very brave woman."

"I'm righting old wrongs," she corrected him. "Courage has little to do with it. Faith, yes. Bravery?" She shook her head and tapped the book with the tabby-striped kitten on the front. "The cat in this book, Debbie, did what she needed to do for her baby to survive. And that's what I'm doing here." She laid her hand atop her rounded abdomen. "And that's what Jasmine did, too. Yes, it took her longer, but I'm going to thank God every day that she made the right choice, because your daughter, Tori, is a pure delight."

Seth stood.

So did Gianna.

"Thank you for telling me all this." He pulled her into an embrace, a hug she'd love to dwell in forever, but that wasn't possible. She enjoyed it for the moment, though, loving the feel of him. His scent. The rugged texture of the well-made Carhartt jacket beneath her cheek. "And I disagree. I think you were amazingly brave and courageous to do this on your own."

"Not on my own. Me and God, this time. And Gram."

She smiled up at him, and he dropped his mouth to hers for one sweet, gentle kiss, a kiss that whispered hope and promise. A promise that could never be, so why was she enjoying the kiss so much? "Seth, I—"

"I've got to go. Carmen was nice to take Tori home so we could talk, but I've got an early day tomorrow. And then a big weekend coming up over here with the grand opening."

"I'm afraid tomorrow's turn of events will make the grand opening seem anticlimactic."

He hiked a brow, and she indicated the wall clock with a thrust of her chin. "In about fourteen hours my mother and one of my aunts arrive at the airport in Erie."

"Whoa. Your mother's quick."

"Warp speed. She grabbed the first ticket she could find when I told her what I'd done. So no matter what the meteorologists say about tomorrow's weather, be prepared Seth. Storm front approaching."

He brushed a gentle kiss across her brow, squeezed her hand and moved to go. But then he turned, and the expression on his face said tough emotions haunted him, as well. "Your husband. Michael. He went to the store to get ice cream for you."

"Mint chocolate chip."

"And he was carrying a gun?"

She met his gaze straight on because this was the truth she needed to face. A truth he needed to face, as well. "Michael was a state trooper. Like my father and grandfather. I lost my dad when I was Tori's age. He was killed while tending an accident scene on a snowy night on an access ramp to the thruway. The last thing I wanted to do was fall in love with a cop, but when I met Michael I threw caution to the wind. And you know the rest of that story."

His face said he understood, but his eyes?

His eyes said he realized why she tried to stay an arm's

length away. Why she pulled back repeatedly when what she longed to do was move forward, into his arms.

She'd lived the double loss of father and husband to the badge. She didn't dare take that chance for her children's sake. This wasn't about statistics or fate, it was about a mother's love and protection, and that was something she didn't take lightly. "Good night, Seth."

"Good night."

She watched him walk away, wanting to chase after him. Talk with him, laugh with him, grow old with him. But in Gianna's life only one of the three men she'd loved lived to grow old, and no way could she take that chance again. But seeing Seth's tall, broad profile as he strode through the cold, damp night, oh, how she wished she could.

CHAPTER THIRTEEN

"G RAM, I CAN PICK UP Mom and Aunt Rose on my own. Why don't you stay here and—"

Carmen's look put a lid on the suggestion as Gianna angled into the driver's seat. She had to slide the seat back a notch to allow room for her growing belly, and Carmen's face softened. "They'll understand, *cara mia.*"

Gianna wished that was true. She sent her grandmother a look of doubt as she turned to back out of the driveway. "Today?"

Carmen's short, tight laugh showed the impossibility of that. "Soon. When they see you all round and lovely. When your mother feels the push of her grandchild's feet. She always comes around. Once she figures out a way to make it her idea. She gets that from your grandpa."

"She must, because you're only like that when you're matchmaking."

"I do not match. I leave that to God." Carmen whisked a tissue from her purse and pulled down the passenger-side mirror to check her hair and makeup as they approached the interstate ramp. "But I'm not afraid to open a window of opportunity as needed."

"In case God forgot how," Gianna offered wryly. She made the turn onto I-86, and her grandmother's laugh helped ease the knot in Gianna's gut.

"God uses His earthly instruments as He sees fit," Carmen replied. "Who am I but a channel of His peace?"

"Try that line with Mom," Gianna advised, but Carmen's snort said she was smarter than that. "At least they're not going to be sleeping on our couch. That would get awkward. And crowded."

"And loud," Carmen muttered. She double-checked her lipstick and must have decided she looked all right because she snapped the little mirror cover closed with a flick of her wrist. "But they mean well, both of them, and it's understandable that they're hurt by our reticence."

"But we gained six months."

Carmen smiled. "Crucial to our overall goal and well-being. And now?" She turned and smiled across the front seat of the car. "We'll keep them so busy helping with the grand opening they'll barely have time to think, much less yell."

"If the weather holds."

Carmen shrugged. "We cannot change the weather. We've done what we can to make the store a success from the beginning, and if we need a little more time?" She raised her shoulders in a shrug. "Then I will dip into your grandfather's legacy. I will consider it my contribution to the local economy."

"Gram, I have money," Gianna protested. As a cop, Michael had made sure she'd be financially protected if something happened to him. "We don't need to—"

"You will need that nest egg for those babies. Your future. Their future." Carmen made a face that said they'd do it her way, no questions asked. "My money would come to you and your brother anyway. Why not here and now while I have the fun of helping you spend it?"

"But what if—"

"What if I get sick? Or need long-term care?"

"Things happen," Gianna reminded her. "It's important for you to be financially secure."

"I will see to all that, and I have insurance for such things. Right now…" She directed her attention to the sign for the Erie International Airport coming up on her right. "We must focus on the current drama."

Gianna pulled in a deep breath as her mother and Aunt Rose pushed through the heavy glass doors by baggage claim a few minutes later. She opened the driver's door, stepped out and moved to greet her mother.

Sofia's gasp pulled her up short.

Aunt Rose followed suit, a hand to her mouth, her eyes trained on Gianna's very pregnant belly.

But then her mother did a most surprising thing. She moved forward, eyes round, but her mouth smiling, and she laid her hands on either side of her daughter's rounded tummy. "Hello, my little darlings, my precious babies. This is your grandma speaking, your *real* one, my sweetests, the one who raised your mama. And I do believe I managed that quite well."

She shot a look at Carmen that said old women should know their place, and Carmen laughed out loud as she hugged Rose. "Your daughter's grace, strength and fortitude do you proud, Sofia. It is clear you and Sal did a very good job."

"Your compliments will get you nowhere with me, Mother." Sofia directed a scathing gaze toward her mother but then sighed and smiled as she reached out to touch the babies one more time. "And you, Gianna? You feel all right? You feel good? No aches? No pains? No agita?"

"I feel wonderful."

"Ach. Youth!" Aunt Rose clasped a hand to her lower back and made a face. "When I carried your cousins I had such pain, such pain! I was not sure if I could do it, but I held on, dear girl, with the help of your uncle, of course, and I don't know how I would have gotten through it without him. Although—" she paused and waggled her head as if indecisive "—I'm not sure he was ever a bit of help once they were born, so whatever! Look at you! You look wonderful. And I said to your mother, 'Sofia,' I said, 'do you think she'll gain a lot of weight like you did? With twins besides?' But I can see now that my worries were for nothing because you are just a lovely weight, don't you think so, Sofia?"

"She looks fine, of course," Sofia shot back. "She looks wonderful, and thank you for sharing with the entire neighborhood around Erie, Pennsylvania's airport that I got fat when I had my babies. Like this entire corner of the world needs to know my business, Rose?"

Rose waved her off as she climbed into the backseat of the car. "Four people, maybe five, heard me, and none of them will ever see you again. But, Gianna! Look at you! So lovely, so beautiful, *bellisima!* I cannot wait to hear all about what you've been doing—"

"What *we've* been doing," Gianna reminded them as Sofia stowed the bags in the trunk. "I couldn't have done any of this—the babies, the new business, the sewing and costuming—without Grandma."

"Indispensable, I'm sure. And taking over the world as we know it in typical fashion." Sofia slanted a cool look at her mother, but Carmen pretended not to notice, and that was the difference between mother and daughter.

Sofia needed to have her say and be declared the victor. She was a have-the-last-word kind of woman.

Grandma quietly forged her path in life, rarely straying, a perfect example of what Gianna wanted to be. But right now? With two disgruntled Italian mothers stewing in her backseat? She'd focus on driving and getting them all back to Kirkwood alive. And that meant sunglasses for the midday glare…

And a hope that Grandma could carry the conversation with her usual grace for the long drive home.

A long drive? How about a long day? Week? Month? Season?

Gianna shoved the thoughts aside. She'd reached a point where she needed to deal with things factually. Honestly. Seth was right; she needed to come clean, so she did.

The fact that both women were staying at the bed-and-breakfast in the village meant the proprietor and anyone within shouting distance would most likely become privy to the entire family's business. Gianna had grown up as a Rinaldi. A part of her was accustomed to the roller-coaster flow.

But was the sleepy town of Kirkwood prepared?

She worried the inside of her cheek as she steered the car back onto I-86, pretty sure Kirkwood Lake hadn't seen the likes of Sofia and Rose before. As she changed lanes, her Bluetooth signaled an incoming call. She smiled at the dashboard readout and hit the button. "Hey, Seth."

"Gianna, I've got both signs in place, but you're most likely going to make me change the one facing east because it looks ridiculous."

"Then change it."

"No argument? No convincing? No explanation of why it looks bad? You trust the judgment of a mere male for your grand opening?"

The total silence in Gianna's backseat meant her mother and aunt were tuned in to the speakerphone conversation, a family reality. Gianna blocked them out and focused on Seth and the road. "I couldn't reach high enough to see how it looked, Seth, so you decide. We'll be back there in about forty-five minutes."

"Then I wish I didn't have to leave in thirty," he remarked, and Gianna didn't have to glance in the rearview mirror to see the ladies' reactions. The heightened electricity in the air was clue enough.

"We'll see you tonight when you pick up Tori."

"I'm working late, so Mom's picking her up and keeping her overnight."

The thought that she wouldn't see Seth today made her realize how much she counted on seeing him. "Tomorrow, then."

"Yes. Gotta go. I want this done before I leave."

"Thanks, Seth."

A moment's hesitation said he was considering what to say, a moment long enough for Gianna to hold her breath—along with the two middle-aged women in the backseat—and then he made the car full of women smile by simply saying, "You're welcome, honey."

"Well." Sofia arched a brow and directed a smile toward Rose as she elongated the single-syllable word.

Rose returned the look with matched satisfaction.

Carmen swallowed a sigh and maintained her silence while Gianna mentally recognized that nothing in her life would be private again. Not for a very long time. Maybe ever. A firm kick from Twin A or B confirmed her suspicion.

But seeing those two little smiles in the backseat, she realized that might not be such a bad thing, after all.

A wise man knows to bring food.

Seth might not be all that wise, but Jenny Campbell didn't raise any dummies either, so he made sure to stop by Seb Walker's bakery in Jamison before his early shift was complete the next day. Seb might not have fancy Italian crème cookies or stuffed cannolis, but his cream puffs were a sight to behold, and his carrot cake? A Campbell family favorite. If he was going to help ease Gianna's mother into her new reality of grandmother, cake couldn't hurt.

The inner door of Gianna's apartment swung open as he walked up the driveway. An older woman stood there, smiling, waving him in as if she knew him, but she didn't, so how—

"Dad! Look who's here! It's Gianna's mother and her aunt!" Tori darted to the door from across the kitchen, and the woman next to her broadened her smile.

"Come in, come in!" She pushed the outer door toward him and stepped back. "You must be Seth. We've heard so much about you! And your daughter, this one!" She grabbed Tori's cheeks between her hands and gave her a smacking kiss. "She is so smart, so funny! And I think she looks like you, no?"

Tori's laughter eased what could have been an awkward moment. "I look like my mother, actually, when she was younger, but I would be okay with looking like Dad. Only not as hairy."

Seth smiled down at her, gave her a half hug and handed the boxes to the older woman. Aunt? Mother?

He had no idea, and when the second one entered the kitchen from the shop area, he was even more confused. "You're twins?"

"No, she is eleven months older." The one from the shop pointed a finger at the other. "And I'm thinner. But people do say we look alike."

"Again with the weight, Rose?"

Rose. Ah. The aunt. Seth nodded to her as she crossed the room, then turned toward the original woman. "Then you must be Gianna's mother."

"Sofia Bianchi Rinaldi." She extended her hand and took a moment to look him over. "Gianna and Joe, they are my family, my bambinos, my darlings."

"I met Joe when Gianna moved in." Seth took off his overcoat and hung it on the back of a chair. In almost perfect unison the Italian women snatched his coat from the back of the chair and made sure it was hung properly in the closet.

He worked to level his expression by the time they

turned back and didn't dare look at Tori's grin. That would be unwise, because if she started laughing, he'd follow along, and somehow he didn't think the middle-aged sisters would see the humor in simultaneous jacket hanging.

"Seth." Gianna came through the connecting curtain, and the look of relief she sent him made him feel good. Real good. He motioned to the shop.

"Are we ready for tomorrow?"

Her face said one thing, her words another. "As ready as we'll ever be."

"You have seen the shop, how nice it is?"

One of the women refocused her attention on him, and he groped for a name, then gave up. "It's beautiful."

"Seth owns the building, Mom. I rent it from him." Gianna's nose twitched. She spotted the boxes, looked up at him and her eyes went bright as if he'd just hung the moon. "Carrot cake?"

"Yes."

"I will be forever in your debt."

"Part of the goal," he quipped back, and pretended not to notice the women's combined approval of their repartee.

"So this building is yours?" The nearest woman directed the question to him.

He nodded. "It was part of my grandmother's legacy. I bought it when prices were down. Fixed it up. It seemed like it belonged in the family."

Appreciation for family and real estate brightened her dark eyes. Seth found himself searching for an identifier to tell the women apart. Mom—*Sofia*—was wearing a striped shirt in shades of purple. Rose's shirt was floral, but in the same shades of purple and green. He wondered if they did that on purpose, or did they both like purple?

"The building is charming," Sofia said. "So you must be the man who has done the work on this lovely place?

You have a fine eye, Seth. The woodwork, the railings, the nautical tones reflect someone who cares deeply."

"Or that was the color my father had on the mismatch table of the local hardware store." Seth shrugged lightly. "But I'll take the credit, Mrs. Rinaldi."

"Sofia. Please. And this is my sister, Rose."

"My pleasure, ma'am." Seth stuck out his hand to Rose, and she dimpled like a schoolgirl. "Gianna, do you need any help tonight?"

She shook her head and hooked a thumb behind her. "Between Tori and Gram we've got all the last-minute stuff done. The coffee service and tea area are set up. The cookies and little cakes are ordered and should arrive by 8:00 a.m. The computerized registers are working, and we have change in the cash drawer. We're good."

"I'll be here first thing, okay?" Tori slipped into her hoodie, grabbed her new backpack and started for the door. Seth cleared his throat and she stopped short and turned. "I'm so happy that our superintendent's conference day is the same as your grand opening, Gianna! Nice to meet you, ladies!"

"And you, too, Tori."

"So nice, honey. Yes!"

"And you're sure there's nothing you need me to do tonight, Gianna?" Seth asked again. "No last-minute errand? I'm glad to be your 'gopher.'"

Gianna considered his offer, then shook her head. "Thank you, but no. We're good. I'm excited and a little nervous that we're finally at this point. Ready to open." She clasped her hands around her rounded tummy, and the look she gave him made him think of old-time movies and vintage TV. Sweet. Lovely. Guileless. "But I'll make sure I keep Tori busy all day tomorrow."

Seth turned to say goodbye to the older women, but they'd disappeared. He swung back, caught Gianna's look of chagrin and choked back a laugh. "They're giving us a moment together."

"One they're no doubt watching and waiting to talk about at length," Gianna said softly.

"It's never good to disappoint mothers." Seth whispered the words with a smile as he swept a kiss to her mouth, then her brow. "Get some rest. Tomorrow you'll be running on adrenaline, but by Sunday you'll crash. Might as well stock up a little tonight."

"Thank you, Seth."

He grinned, touched a finger to her cheek, then turned to go. "Good night, ladies." He called the words toward the living room, and Rose stuck her head out, feigning surprise.

"Oh, you're going? Yes, good night, so nice to meet you."

"Yes, lovely, Seth!"

The second voice sounded from deeper in the room, but Seth was a good cop with strong instincts, and his intuition was telling him that these two women were firmly in his corner, even from a distance. And he was okay with that.

Seth figured out two things by Friday afternoon. First, that Gianna's mother and aunt talked at a decibel level that made the Campbells sound like an ancient tribe of nomadic whisperers.

Second?

They carried hearts of gold alongside their well-used lungs.

Once the doors were opened and people streamed in from the surrounding towns, he backed off to his cold yard across the street. He opened his driveway to parking. He kept small children amused while their mothers shopped. And the steady stream of plain brown vintage bags coming out of the store said their Friday opening was a hit.

If Saturday followed suit?

Gianna and Carmen could count this venture as an initial success, with nine months before another cold, low-population winter took hold. Retailers in the north counted on spring, summer and fall to get them through winter. With the babies due, he knew Gianna wouldn't be able to produce as much handmade clothing. Would she be able to find enough to keep the shelves filled?

He hoped so. His phone rang midday and he picked it up. "Hey, Mom."

"I'm across the street at Vintage Place and having the time of my life," Jenny Campbell declared.

Seth groaned on purpose. "I do believe Addie and Cass both said to avoid the puffed-sleeve display."

Jenny's voice tipped up in glee. "I bought three. I love puffed sleeves!"

"We know, Mom. We all know."

"For your information, they're coming back in style, so you hush," she scolded. "And I've seen your closet, Seth. I don't think you're in any position to criticize."

He grinned at his end of the phone because his mother was correct. He liked looking all right, he supposed. But it wasn't something he gave a lot of thought to.

"Anyway, Tori is having the time of her life. She's got a great outfit on—"

"Gianna put it together for her."

Jenny's voice said that was no surprise. "Well, it looks wonderful. And the hip scarf she's sporting? Seth, she's growing up."

He knew that. Dreaded it. But nature wasn't interested in his abject fear of puberty. "She's beautiful, isn't she?"

"Gianna or Tori?"

Her spontaneous question made him laugh. "Both."

"Then, yes. I brought food for later so you guys can celebrate and not cook. And I met Sofia and Rose."

"Did they steamroll you?"

"They're marvelous! I did make a surreptitious call to have a hearing check set up for Monday, but I most likely needed one anyway."

Seth laughed again. "Thanks for coming into town, Mom. And shopping. Gianna needs to make money if she's going to pay my inflated rent and turn a profit."

Jenny came out the door of the shop, waved her phone in the air at him and hoisted two full shopping bags from the sidewalk across the street. "My pleasure, dear!"

He waved back as she climbed into her car and edged away from the illegal parking spot she'd grabbed. In season, the sheriffs would have to ticket folks for parking in the wrong spots, but now? Mid-March? Everyone was glad for some economic upswing and an influx of people.

At lunchtime he toted a loaded pizza into the apartment side of the Vintage Place building and parked it on the kitchen table.

By suppertime he'd removed bags of winter tree-fall and debris from his yard, power washed the garage door and kept an easy watch across the street. As closing time drew near, he cleaned up, put on fresh clothes and headed across the street with twin bottles of sparkling grape juice to celebrate.

As he started up the driveway a car pulled in next to him. A woman climbed out of the driver's seat, barely gave him a glance and moved toward the shop door.

"The shop just closed, ma'am." Seth's voice drew her attention and when she turned, the face she gave him said shopping didn't make the short list.

"I'm looking for Gianna Costanza."

Seth read the look, the posture, the tone, and kept his voice even. "For?"

"None of your business. Is she here?"

Whoa. This woman needed an attitude adjustment. Her voice rankled him. Her tough stance put his defenses on high alert. She drew her shoulders back, brought her chin up, and he was pretty sure she was about to take another solid verbal aim at him when the side porch door swung open. "Dad! Come on in. Grandma brought food and we had the best day ever!"

Gianna appeared at Tori's side, and Seth watched her face transform as she spotted him, then the woman off to his side. She paled and her throat convulsed. "Marie."

"You didn't think to tell me?"

The woman marched forward and Seth kept pace, ready to remove any threat to Gianna, but first he handed off the two glass bottles to Tori. A single firm look sent the girl back inside, and he was glad she obeyed the silent order.

"You do this." She sent a hard stare at Gianna's abdomen, then drew her gaze up slowly. "And you think it is all right to leave Michael's mother out of the equation? You think to have my grandchildren and I have no right to know? Why is this, Gianna, when I have given you nothing but love for all these years, both before losing my precious son and after?"

"Marie, come in, it's cold. And I'll explain."

"Explain?" She directed a tough look over Gianna's shoulder. Carmen stood there, arms crossed, an eyebrow thrust up, and Seth was pretty sure these women had faced off before. And equally sure Carmen had won. "And your part in all this, Carmen Bianchi? You think you can wave your bony little arm and we all fall into line because you are the matriarch, the wonderful grandma who knows all while the rest of us count for nothing? Well, this is what I say to that." She made a weird spitting noise toward the ground. "You are in charge of nothing, Carmen. Not with me or my family, and these babies are as much Costanza as they are Bianchi and Rinaldi. And therefore as much mine as yours."

Seth had never seen Gianna angry. He'd have thought she didn't have much practice, but she drew herself up as Marie challenged Carmen, and when she spoke, everyone listened. "They're mine." She took a step forward, and while Seth wouldn't have thought a five-foot-three-inch woman could intimidate, this one did. "I am their mother. I am the one who says what happens and when it happens. They are my flesh and blood and I'm the one who went through years of treatments to make this possible, so don't think for a minute I'm going to let these precious babies be immersed in some sort of family feud."

"They are my son's children." Marie braced herself and laced her voice with steel. "I have rights, Gianna. And connections. You should have never left me out of this."

Seth stepped in before Carmen could. "Are you threatening these ladies, ma'am? Because it's against the law to threaten folks here."

"I'm not threatening, I'm making a solemn pledge," she retorted. "And I'll finish my say while you run along and get the law."

Seth drew out his wallet and flashed his I.D. "I am the law. So let me make a suggestion before you go any further." He stayed calm but moved a full step closer, making sure his size didn't go unnoticed. "Why don't you go rest up wherever you're staying and come back tomorrow night after the grand opening sale. We can talk calmly then."

"We? 'We' is nothing to you, you are no part of this." Marie pointed toward Gianna and her grandmother. "Why don't you—"

"Marie. Really." Carmen aimed her gaze at Gianna's rounded form, then agreed with Seth. "You know more than most how fragile Gianna has been. It's cold and late and you're tired from your trip. Get some rest, and we'll talk about this tomorrow."

Marie stood silent and still, staring at Gianna and Carmen, and then she did the unthinkable in Seth's book.

She began to weep.

Her face crumpled. Her hands shook. Tears flowed faster than a spring rain on O'Shaughnessy Creek.

Carmen didn't step forward to offer comfort. Neither did Gianna. After a few awkward seconds, Seth put a hand to the woman's shoulder. "May I walk you to your car? Please?"

She nodded, head down, deflated.

Seth accompanied her to the car, and when she had buckled her seat belt, he leaned down. "Are you okay to drive, Mrs. Costanza?"

"I am fine. I am hurt and rejected by those who should know better, but that is no big surprise. And I have only to drive over there." She pointed to the bed-and-breakfast a few doors down from Seth. Seth decided he better call the sheriff's substation and put out a special alert because Gianna's mother and aunt were staying in the same B and B. He just hoped none of them had a license to carry a concealed weapon, although Marie's long, bright red fingernails appeared fairly dangerous and possibly lethal.

Marie turned more fully his way. "What is your interest in my daughter-in-law?"

Seth wasn't a big talker, and he didn't like personal, probing questions. "My daughter is learning to sew. And she's helping in the store. Gianna and Carmen have been very good to her."

His explanation appeared to mollify Marie slightly, but then he saw the look she cast at the now-empty doorway. Anger, mistrust and hurt darkened her expression, and intuition told him she was no stranger to those feelings. Which meant they may have been directed at Gianna in the past.

She thrust the car into gear, backed up slowly and drove the short distance to the gingerbread-style lodging house on the left. He didn't follow her to see if she needed help with her bags. He turned and walked into Gianna's apartment, pretty sure Marie's unexpected arrival had thrown a wet blanket on the day's celebration.

Sofia was scolding Carmen.

Carmen was fixing Gianna a cup of tea.

Rose was fluttering about, trying to ease the tensions and causing more with her constant chatter.

Only Tori seemed at ease with all the back-and-forth. As Seth walked through the door, the twelve-year-old held up her hands and gave a time-out signal. "Stop. Please."

Gianna seemed surprised, but her expression said she welcomed the kid's interruption. Carmen willingly turned an expectant ear Tori's way. Rose and Sofia seemed taken aback by the girl's vehement direction, but they also went quiet.

Temporarily.

"My dad says you've got to sort things through in your head and then take them to God." She met the ladies' gazes with one sweep of the room. "So all the talking in the world isn't going to fix this tonight, right? And we have all this good food, and Dad brought sparkling stuff, and we had the best day ever! And I had more fun than I ever thought I would today, so can we *not* fight tonight? Just celebrate, like we planned?"

Gianna's lips twitched, and when they did, Carmen's followed suit. "A moratorium on fighting, arguing and all things negative. That gets my vote."

"Mine, too." Gianna smiled at Tori, reached out and embraced her in a big hug. "And you were marvelous today, honey. Amazing, really."

"I had so much fun!" Tori's face reflected the truth of the statement. "Helping people find things. Telling them what looked nice. Packing their bags. Rehanging clothes."

"You had fun rehanging clothes?" Seth moved farther into the room, glad the tension had been broken. "I've seen your bedroom, Tor. Why do I find this hard to believe?"

She burst out laughing. "I like rehanging clothing over here." She stressed the location and waved to the store with her right hand. "Gianna, do you need help with the stew?"

"Mom made stew?" Seth moved closer and inhaled deeply. "I am a very happy man."

"And fresh bread. And a broccoli salad."

"She is a kind woman, your mother." Carmen reached up a hand to his cheek briefly. "Like mother, like son."

"Except Dad doesn't cook all that well," Tori told them. "He tries, but I figure as I get older, I can help out with cooking more. Because I have more time," she added hurriedly, as if afraid she'd hurt Seth's feelings.

"I'm all for that." Seth ruffled her hair. "Anything that lessens my workload gets a resounding 'yes' from my corner."

"I'll get the plates." Rose moved to the far cupboard.

"And I'll put out the silverware." Sofia opened the drawer adjacent to the sink. Those two normal gestures dropped tensions further, and as the group gathered to eat Jenny Campbell's delicious meal, the emotional strain lessened. But from the look in Carmen's eye every time her gaze strayed to the east-facing window—and Gianna's square-shouldered posture that said she was ready for battle—Seth was pretty sure they were enjoying a brief respite from all-out family-drama engagement.

CHAPTER FOURTEEN

G IANNA COULDN'T HELP BUT OVERHEAR the two-way conversation the following morning.

"Rose said she might have mentioned Gianna's condition to Genevieve Peccoraro before we left Florida, but she's sure Genevieve would never tell a soul something she shared in strictest confidence. She's too good a friend for that."

"Then how do you suppose Marie came to know of the babies?" Carmen's voice stayed flat with disbelief. "Genevieve was most likely on the phone to Marie before your plane left the ground. They've always been close. When they're not bickering. And Genevieve probably couldn't wait to brag that she knew something before Marie. It has always been that way with them."

Gianna walked down the stairs with a pretense of calm. She wished she could ignore the conversation between her grandmother and mother, but she'd instigated the whole mess by her deceit, so it was up to her to straighten things out.

She'd prayed last night. For strength, for forgiveness, for the right words to soothe Marie's hurt feelings. The fact that Marie's feelings rumpled easily was understood, but Gianna hadn't intended her to find out about the twins in this roundabout fashion. She joined the two women, poured a cup of coffee because she was sick to death of tea and turned to face them. "I hurt her. I'll fix it."

"She is too sensitive." Sofia raised her hand, dismissive. "It is preposterous to carry on so."

"You were upset, too, Mom."

"Me, yes. I am your mother, and your grandmother takes special liberties with you. She loves being the favorite, the best 'Nonna.' That grows old after a while."

Carmen's lips twitched. "I can't say I'm against the favoritism, Sofia. I enjoy my granddaughter's love very much."

Sofia faced her. "Bah. You enjoy being in charge more than anything, and my daughter is more like you than me. That is all right except when we forget that *I* am the mother. And although we do not do things the same way—" she settled a stern look on Gianna and Carmen "—or think the same way, I do not deserve to be left out of things. I understand why you did this." She turned her attention more fully to Gianna. "I get excited, and I worry. I worry loudly. Your grandmother does not. But when I am done being excited and worried, I am filled with joy. Like now." She hugged Gianna, and the feel of her mother's arms around her helped loosen the nasty knot of emotions within. "Of course, I am mostly pleased because my blabbermouth sister is stuck across the street trying to be nice to Marie, and that is her penance for telling Genevieve about your condition."

Carmen acknowledged Sofia's words with a look of acceptance as she began opening pastry boxes of fresh cookies and tiny cakes. "Then the punishment fits the crime."

"On this we agree." Sofia budged her way into the table area and pointed toward the shop. "You two know what needs to be done in there. I do not. But I can put together pretty trays of sweets. And I like that your young man brought us cake the other night. He is thoughtful, that one."

"He is," Gianna agreed. "But he is not my young man."

"Perhaps I should say 'significant other'? Or 'special friend'?" Her mother's frank expression said she wasn't buying Gianna's rebuttal. "In any case, his daughter is a dream child, and I could just sit and chatter with her all day. So full of life and joy, and so smart!"

Sofia's description inspired a shared smile between Gianna and Carmen. Tori was blossoming day by day. The assurance that she could stay with Seth, her joy of working in the store and with fabric, and her gradually increasing school skills seemed to feed her rocky self-esteem.

"She's a sweet one." Carmen picked up her coffee and headed into the shop area. "I'm going to run a hem on that dress for Mrs. Yardley. I should be able to get it done before we open."

"And I'll double-check tags and make sure everything's in its rightful place." Gianna looped an arm around her mother's waist and leaned in to kiss her cheek. "Thank you for doing this, Mom."

Her mother's happy grunt was answer enough. Gianna glanced across the street before she stepped into the shop. On one side of Overlook Drive was Seth's house, warm and welcoming. Down the road, visible behind unleafed spreading oaks and maples, the green, pink and yellow bed-and-breakfast looked just as inviting, but Gianna had seen the look on Marie's face the night before, and it brought back a pincushion's worth of prickly memories.

She'd tolerated Marie's bossiness when she and Mike were married because she needed to. And the fourteen-mile distance from their home to hers had offered leeway.

But she'd moved here because she understood the woman's emotional overload, not from any intent to keep these babies from their paternal grandmother. And Marie's feelings, once hurt, tended to linger in the abyss, which meant she'd have to coax her former mother-in-law back into the fold.

Michael hadn't needed to bow and scrape. As her only son, he could do no wrong in his mother's eyes. But trying to live up to the standard set by an overbearing mother-in-law had taught Gianna to smile and nod, then do what she thought best. It had worked years ago, with Michael as a buffer. But now?

She organized dresses with quick hands, certain the smile-and-nod trick of old wouldn't cut it anymore. She finished up the racks as the doorbell rang on the apartment side of the building. She turned, surprised, because no one ever used the doorbell.

Her mother came through the curtained partition. In her arms was a glorious basket of flowers, a tribute to spring in bright pinks, yellows, purples and greens. Airy white baby's breath peeked from between the blossoms, contrasting the fuller blooms with an artist's touch. "That's gorgeous."

"Stunning." Carmen's eyebrows rose as she looked from the basket to Sofia. "And it is from?"

"The nonsignificant other." Sofia jerked her head in the direction of Seth's house as Gianna cleared vintage prints of yesteryear Hollywood stars from an antique side table. She set the basket down and withdrew a small white envelope from the plastic holder. "The card."

Gianna took the tiny card from her mother's hand, opened it and read, "Congratulations on a great yesterday, a better today and a blessed tomorrow. It's kind of nice to have you in Kirkwood. And right across the street." It was signed Seth and Tori and the words *a blessed tomorrow* filled her with heightened self-confidence. She'd made it this far. She'd done well. With God's help, her family's blessing and great new neighbors, she'd be fine. She pushed thoughts of the evening's confrontation out of her mind and concentrated on the here and now.

Her mother placed an arm around her shoulders, her voice matter-of-fact. "For a friend, this man does okay."

Carmen met Sofia's cryptic look from across the room. "In my day he'd be considered a 'keeper,' but then I'm old, and things were no doubt different." Her expression said Gianna should be considered certifiable for keeping a guy like Seth Campbell at arm's length, but then Grandma had been with the love of her life for forty years before he'd passed away from natural causes.

"Stop. Both of you." Gianna turned and sent them a look meant to shush with little hope it would happen. "I buried my father as a kid. I buried my husband as a bride. The idea of putting these two babies in the line of fire, of taking a chance for them to go through that pain and loss by deliberately dating a cop, is beyond contemplation. I know you both mean well. And I know you both love me, but you have to understand this—from where I'm standing, nothing can come of this attraction to Seth Campbell. I can't risk burying another policeman I love, or intentionally doing that to my children. It isn't going to happen."

"But…" A deep voice came through from just beyond the curtain. "You like the flowers."

Her heart stopped cold in her chest.

Seth had walked in during her scolding. He'd been in the kitchen, separated by nothing more than a sheet of calico cotton. He'd most likely overheard everything.

If she had a trapdoor mechanism for the floor to swallow her up, Gianna would push it right now. Because she didn't, she turned, ready to face off with Seth and apologize for hurting him.

He came into the room, holding one tiny guest cake while eating another, and he aimed a look of approval at the basket. "They did great. So. You like 'em?"

His calm wasn't forced. He wasn't taken aback or insulted. He seemed…

Fine. He seemed fine, when he'd just overheard her saying how there could be nothing between them, ever. Why was he fine when her insides were under attack trying to figure out a way to fix things? She mustered a breath and nodded. "They're beautiful. Thank you, Seth."

"You're welcome." He didn't hesitate, didn't glance around, didn't miss a beat, just swept one arm around her and kissed her soundly, then took a step back as if that was an expected thing to do. "I've got to help my father today, but just so we're clear?"

There was no turning away from those blue eyes, eyes that could be soft and beseeching, then turn hard and decisive as needed. "Yes?"

"Campbell men don't give up easy. Ever."

Sofia put a hand to her heart, clearly impressed.

Eyes down, Carmen pretended to be working on the already hemmed garment, but her grin said Seth Campbell had gone up another rung on her estimation ladder.

Tori came in just then, and Gianna bit back what she might have said, because in truth? Seth's declaration made her feel like things could be all right, given time. Yes, she understood all the reasons why she shouldn't fall head over heels in love with the big, blue-eyed blond. But when he talked like that? Gave her that look? Kissed her?

None of it mattered.

Marie walked into the store thirty minutes before closing time. They'd had a busy morning and a busier afternoon. The fair weather helped, and with a storm predicted for Sunday, Gianna knew she'd been fortunate to have a sweet spring weekend for the opening.

She watched quietly as Marie moved around the store.

When Marie noticed Gianna standing in the back, she made no sound or gesture of acknowledgment, but her flat expression and silence spoke across the thirty feet separating them. Disapproval and disappointment. She kept her purse high on her shoulder and tucked against her waist, untrusting the local clientele. She checked price tags and sniffed audibly, insulted.

It wasn't the prices she found repulsive. Gina knew her well enough to see beyond the obvious. It was the thought of wearing someone else's clothes and paying for the dubious honor. And even though the store was carrying three distinct lines of new vintage-styled clothing, the gently used clothing racks had drawn great interest from the weekend shoppers. Which meant a lot of Kirkwood Lake folks didn't share Marie's repugnance of someone else's castoffs.

Mrs. Thurgood came into the store shortly before closing time. The elderly woman from the east side of the lake marched through the store and brandished a used cord-handled gift bag that had seen better days. "For you!" Delight colored the older woman's voice as she handed the bag to Gianna. "And those babies! I thought I might be too busy to make these over spring, so I wanted to finish them up before I started more things for the summer festival season. Mind, I've got a lot done," she added, lest anyone overhearing her might think she'd been shirking over the elongated winter, "but taking time out to make something special for these babies was pure pleasure!"

"Mrs. Thurgood, thank you." Gianna hugged her, surprised and delighted. "May I open it now?"

"Yes. Please. And tell me what you think. I know Carmen said you're having a boy and a girl, so I wanted them different but similar. If that makes any sense."

"Perfect sense," declared Sofia as she walked through the fabric divider. "Oh, Gianna, how precious."

"It is." Gianna lifted a miniature white christening gown knit with the softest of yarns. Blue trim marked the hem and thin blue satin ribbon wove an in-and-out pattern through the wrist openings. "Oh, it's just simply amazing, Mrs. Thurgood. So delicate and perfect."

Mrs. Thurgood's face said Gianna's reaction made her day. She nodded to the bag Gianna had set down near the cash register. "And the other one?"

Gianna withdrew a matching gown, trimmed in pink, but not the typical soft baby-pink. This was a full-toned raspberry, one of Gianna's favorite shades. She turned toward Mrs. Thurgood, wondering, and the woman smiled fondly.

"You wear that color often. That's how I knew. And if this baby girl has her mother's coloring, then this shade of pink will be just right, don't you think?"

"Stunning." Gianna reached out and hugged her again. "I love them, Mrs. Thurgood. I'm overwhelmed because I know how long it takes to make things like this."

"Not so long when time is all you've got and winter hangs on well past its welcome," returned the widow. "Like your grandma, I keep myself busy. And making these little gowns?" She grinned, her pleasure evident in a wreath of wrinkles. "A true delight. I hope you don't mind me reusing that bag." She touched the frayed gift bag with one hand. "I don't hold with waste and I'm known to be frugal, so I like to reuse things as often as possible." She sent a look around the vintage store and smiled. "I knew you were the kind of folks who'd understand that logic."

"Use it up, wear it out," Carmen agreed. She put her hand on Mrs. Thurgood's shoulder. "You have blessed us like you bless this community with goodness and sharing."

Mrs. Thurgood shrugged off the compliment, but joy showed in her face, her smile. "I must get off. We've got a project to talk about at the church hall, and I don't like to do these things on Saturday night, but with the bicentennial celebrations coming up, even an old duck like me has to make exceptions. Good night, dear." She pressed Gianna's hand and hurried out of the store.

A murmur of approval went through the few remaining customers. Smiles were exchanged over the beauty of baby clothing.

Gianna pretended not to notice Marie's frown. She kept her attention focused on the customers, half hoping closing time lingered. And it did as they finished up the last sale of the day, but keeping Marie at bay might have made matters worse. From the look on her face, Gianna was pretty sure that was the case.

CHAPTER FIFTEEN

"YOU HAVE BROKEN MY HEART. And you have done so deliberately." Marie pushed forward from her side of the small kitchen table, her eyes boring into Gianna's a short time later. She'd exchanged her customary melodrama for hard-edged anger, and Gianna wondered which side she disliked more.

Both, she decided, wishing she saw the softer side of Marie more often. "My intent wasn't to hurt anyone," she began, but Marie waved a hand, brushing her words aside.

"Bah!"

The typical Marie shutdown made Gianna cringe internally. If Marie didn't agree with you, she refused to listen, but if the Italian matriarch wanted to have a nurturing relationship with her grandchildren, she'd better start listening. And being nice. Soon. "Marie."

Michael's mother kept her face averted, so Gianna touched her sleeve with a gentle hand. "Look at me. Please."

Marie huffed, then turned slightly, as if doing Gianna a favor. In her turn, Gianna bit back a sigh of resignation that would do neither of them any good. "We both lost something precious when Michael died."

"You think I don't know this? That my son, my precious son, was taken from me so callously? While he was out to get ice cream for his pregnant bride at that hour of night? Tell me something I don't know, Gianna. Tell me something that makes this—" She waved a hand toward the rounded swell of Gianna's belly "—all right. To bear my grandchildren without a word to me."

"If you stop scolding, I will explain." Gianna kept her voice taut and her gaze firm, a trait she'd learned from Carmen. *Act calm but be strong.* "For years I've been paying the fertility clinic to keep our last embryos in storage. That wasn't a secret. You all knew we couldn't conceive in the normal way and that we sought help. And you also knew that both pregnancies ended badly."

Marie shrugged concession but didn't look mollified.

"Last year I started thinking about them." Gianna laid her hand atop the babies. "Those last two embryos, and how we'd created them for our own selfish purposes."

"Wanting a child is not selfish. It is normal. Don't call my son names, Gianna. Not in my presence."

"We *were* selfish," Gianna continued, ignoring the interruption. "We thought first of our wants, our needs. So when Michael was shot and I lost that baby, we'd come to a fork in the road. My life changed that month. Your life changed. We all grieved for a loss we shared, but I realized last year that those two tiny scraps of life were living in cryogenic limbo. They had no choice in the matter. They had no say in their creation or their disposal. Should I go on keeping them frozen forever? Or should I cancel payment to the clinic and have them discarded? Or—" she reached out and sandwiched Marie's left hand "—should I offer them the one chance at life God gives? Should I give them my body as an incubator and my love as their shield? What choice did I really have, when you look at it from their point of view?"

"But you tell no one? Except for Carmen? How is that right?"

Gianna kept her voice matter-of-fact. "I lost two pregnancies before. Why get everyone excited or nervous for something that might not work? And frankly, you all tend to overreact to everything. You. My mother. My aunts." Gianna shrugged. "Grandma doesn't. She listens, talks and prays. She stands guard quietly. She helps, but doesn't interfere. I needed someone calm and steady to see me through this, and Michael wasn't available."

Marie's eyes darkened, then brightened with tears.

"I didn't have his strength and grace this time," Gianna continued. "There was no knight in shining armor to run to the store for me late at night, and if you're harboring old feelings about my guilt in all this, you needn't bother. I've regretted letting him go to that store for years, because if I hadn't whined about ice cream, my husband would still be alive."

Marie's face shadowed. She sighed deeply. "I'm wrong to think things like that, Gianna. I'm wrong to look for blame, but after my husband walked out on us, I had no one but Michael. Nothing but Michael. I had no great passion for a career." She indicated the vintage store with a glance in that direction. "No great talent like sewing or painting. I had money." She shrugged. "My father's money. The only thing I had was Michael. He was it, my one and only. *Mi famiglia.* And now you've gone and done this—" she waved her hand toward the obvious pregnancy and the town beyond "—moved here, to take more family from me. And I can't let that pass."

"And yet you must." Gianna sat straighter and met Marie's gaze. "I needed a fresh start. I wanted a new location where I can walk the streets and people see Gianna, not Michael's widow. I want the unceasing talk of my sanity while I grieved the loss of my husband and babies behind me. I can have that here. It would be an impossibility back in Edgerton." She stood and offered the silent message that the conversation was coming to an end. "We don't have to figure all this out now. We have months yet. You are my children's grandmother—"

"Their nonnie."

Gianna acknowledged the sweet name with a dip of her chin. "Their nonnie. But I am their mother, and you need to come to peace with my decisions as their mother. I want them surrounded by love and laughter. Warmth and grace. The faith of our fathers. And I can have all that here with a new, unfettered reputation."

"And what of *their* father? His grave? His monument? How will they know of him, what a fine man he was? How will they respect his courage and bravery? His dedication to others?"

This line of questioning was easy to answer. Gianna reached out and hugged Michael's mother and whispered, "Because we will tell them, Marie. We will show them pictures and tell them stories, and they will realize what a fine and honorable man their father was."

Her words eased the strain but didn't stem Marie's grief. As she moved to the door she turned back, reenergized and seemingly as angry as ever. "You think you can make this all right with pretty words and Judas's kiss, but you cannot. You have stirred my grief with your actions. My life had moved on, I made changes that suit me, and now you've brought that awful loss back to the forefront of my brain, my very consciousness. The night of that phone call, the day of his burial, the empty weeks and months that followed. I had come to grips with it, and now you go behind my back and bring it all up again. I'm not so sure you thought of others when you made this decision. I'm fairly certain you thought of yourself and your emptiness. And maybe that's the part that is unfair. Fatherless children are nothing to be taken lightly."

Harsh words from a bitter person. Gianna held her ground. "A fact I know from experience, making me even more capable of handling this."

"As you handled grief?" Marie's face went hard and cool. "And loss?" She aimed a chilled look at Gianna's abdomen. "Who will be their mama when you fall apart the next time?"

The arrow hit sharp, maybe because Gianna hadn't realized how deep Marie's anger went. Now she knew. "Good night, Marie."

Marie didn't return the farewell. She strode out, walked up the street in the direction of the bed-and-breakfast, and Gianna gripped the edge of the table in the sudden silence, wondering if Marie's prediction would be proved right. Would she fall apart in a crisis? Would pain or grief be her downfall forever, and would her children pay for her shortsightedness? Maybe she wasn't as strong as she made out. Maybe—

No.

She refused to accept Marie's criticism as valid. Grief was normal. It was part of life. And no one should put a limit on feelings, on sorrow, any more than they do on joy. What part of the human equation said it was okay to judge when others have grieved too much or too long? What gave anyone the right to find her lacking?

She sank into the kitchen chair and bowed her head, remembering the psalm she loved so well, a song of David.

You have searched me, Lord, and You know me. You know when I sit and when I rise; You perceive my thoughts from afar. You discern my going out and my lying down; You are familiar with all my ways.

Before a word is on my tongue, You, Lord, know it completely.

You hem me in behind and before, and You lay Your hand upon me. Such knowledge is too wonderful for me, too lofty for me to attain.

God hemmed her in, He watched over her, protecting her. The gracious words meant a great deal to a seamstress.

Once everything else is complete in a garment, the hem must be done to perfection, even and true, a perfect circle.

Like a wedding band.

A soft, familiar knock sounded at the door. When she stood, Seth came into the room, and one look at her face had him hold out his arms. She stepped into his hug, knowing she didn't need his strength to uphold her but wanting it anyway.

Marie had made an accurate if mean-spirited point. Gianna hadn't handled grief with aplomb. She'd been down and out for a long time, but things were different now. Two hearts beat beneath hers, two innocents, whose lives she'd created and now nurtured to fruition.

Could she risk losing this gentle man whose arms wrapped her in a hug that said forever? She'd learned the hard way that forever didn't exist, and now she had two children to care for. Did she dare take a chance on love, knowing the dangers of police work firsthand?

Not in good conscience. And right now, with nearly three months of pregnancy remaining, and a new business blooming, she couldn't think straight enough to see the long road. But the short road said she needed to cool things with Seth Campbell no matter how much her heart said otherwise.

"Dad! Spring!"

Seth turned to face Tori as warm air and the higher pitch of the sun bathed his lungs a week later. Daffodil nubs poked green spikes up from his south-facing front yard. The shade of the house kept the backyard soil cooler, so those bulbs would be weeks behind, but seeing these sprouts of green, and a tuck of tiny crocuses Tori had just spotted, felt good.

"You ready, kid?"

Tori hesitated, then nodded. "I guess."

"Let's go." They were meeting with the principal, the guidance counselor and Tori's teacher today to plan a course of action. Seth read the anxiety in her face, and a similar angst in her gestures, but he couldn't go soft. They needed a plan to catch Tori up with her classmates if she wanted to maintain her grade level. And she needed to be totally invested in the plan.

Right now that didn't seem likely.

But two hours later he left the school, impressed by their professionalism and Tori's composure. He gripped a folder in his hand, the name of a tutor and an outline of what Tori needed to accomplish by September.

He faced her as they reached the car. He raised the folder aloft. "Doable?"

"Yes. I think it is, Dad." Then she smiled, looking much more relaxed than she had two hours before. "I know it is."

His smile matched hers. "That's my girl. I'll give this tutor a call."

"Can't Gianna do it? Please? We work so well together."

They did, but Gianna's current stress and workload made him waver. And her actions this past week said she'd taken a firm step back from the growing attraction between them.

Could he ask? Better yet, *should* he? Tori's imploring look said he needed to, even if the answer wasn't what she hoped. "I'll ask, but we have to be prepared for her to say no, Tori. She's crazy busy even with Carmen's help. The store is off to a great start, which means a whole lot of behind-the-scenes work."

"Like?"

"Ordering. Sewing. Alterations. Shopping online. Books." Tori frowned and Seth explained, "Business accounts. Debit and credit sheets. Figuring things in. Logging expenses. And if people bring things in to sell on consignment, that makes a chain of paperwork, too."

"Well, her computer program does most of the accounting stuff," Tori explained. "Gianna showed me how the software keeps track of all sales, what they've used, what they need to order and what folks are trending on. That way she can target her customers without counting a thing."

Seth hadn't realized such a thing existed, but it made perfect sense. Integrated technology used to be a big deal. Now it was expected. "That might all be true, but she could still be too busy. Just don't set yourself up for disappointment. Okay?"

"Okay."

She agreed to keep him happy, but he saw her face. She was counting on Gianna. As an adult, Seth read his neighbor's time frame with more accuracy than his daughter. The store opening and the influx of family had turned the dynamics of Gianna's afternoons inside out. Seth couldn't see how tutoring would fit into the mix.

"Tori." Gianna looked at the tutoring schedule and frowned, dismayed. "I wish I could, honey, but there's no way I can do this the way it should be done right now."

Grandma made a sound from the other side of the curtain, a noise Gianna knew well. Roughly translated, her grandmother was calling her out with a well-placed grunt.

Gianna ignored her and faced Tori and Seth. "I hate saying no."

"But we—" Seth put a hand on Tori's shoulder "— understand completely. The store is open now, and it's busy."

"Yes. Exactly." Gianna grasped his understanding and ran with it. "Between the store and my family—"

Seth pulled Tori a touch closer, just enough to show his support for his daughter, his unfailing love, a love that withstood the test of time, faith and separation. Turning her back on a chance at that love? At that devotion?

How stupid was she?

And how badly will you feel if the unthinkable happens to Seth and you've gone into this with your eyes wide-open? What makes you think you're strong enough to handle such a possibility? And why would anyone who's lived this scenario twice contemplate putting her children through it?

Doubt gnawed at her. Images of her old self, depressed and grief-stricken, pressed in. She pushed them aside, but not before they'd made their point. She couldn't afford to take chances. Not now. Not ever. What would happen to her children if she fell apart again? That thought alone pushed her further from the invitation in Seth Campbell's blue eyes.

"They did give us the name of a local tutor," Seth said. "We'll give her a call and see what we can set up."

He turned to go, one arm slung around Tori's disappointed shoulders. As they moved toward one door, Marie came in through the other. She tapped her watch as she approached Gianna, and her voice made her time crunch quite clear. "I'm leaving for home now. I understand you're coming home for Easter."

She said it as a command, not a question, but since Gianna had already told the family that she and Gram would drive to Edgerton for Easter weekend, Marie's take wasn't all that important. "Yes."

"I'm contacting my Realtor when I get back. He'll have possibilities for you to consider when you're back home. While all this is nice, Gianna, we both know you don't need to work."

Gianna sucked a breath. Financially, that was true. Michael's insurance had left her comfortable. Mentally?

She needed the push of everyday normal, the art of creativity flowing through her fingers as she made new garments or repaired dated ones. "Gram and I love what we're doing here." She kept her voice mild, and that ease made Marie think she could push further.

"A job which could be done anywhere," Marie stated smoothly. "And not one that has to be located more than five hours away from family, the very people who are willing to pick you up when you fall down."

She clipped the final seven words staccato-style, aiming verbal arrows at Gianna's ego. Gianna dodged the mental jabs and realized she had to give serious thought and prayer to Marie's influence on small children. Gianna had no intention of letting the twins be inundated with negativity. Grace, warmth and wisdom, yes.

And cookies. Cookies were a given.

But this chronic defeatism from Marie?

Not a chance. "Thankfully there's Gram," she said lightly, knowing it would tweak Marie's ire but not really caring.

"And friends." Seth's voice deepened the unnecessary drama. "We're right across the street if you need anything, Gianna."

His voice warmed her. His smile bolstered her flagging ego. His gaze said he believed in her, no matter what, but the fact that he was a cop made her more than nervous. It made her remember. "Thank you, Seth."

He left and Marie moved forward. "You're interested in him."

Gianna was not about to discuss her feelings for Seth with Michael's mother. That went beyond weird. "He's my neighbor and my landlord, and his daughter is a sweetheart who loves to help me here. That's the kind of neighborhood this is. The kind of town this is, Marie."

"You have feelings for him," Marie repeated, as if Gianna hadn't spoken. "While you carry my son's children. This man, this deputy sheriff—" She stressed *deputy* as if it was a bad thing, and then *sheriff* because she didn't believe local police held a candle to state troopers. Fortunately the police in Kirkwood Lake didn't embrace old-school mind-sets. Terrorist attacks across the country had pushed policing departments to a position of teamwork, a positive change. "He cares for his ex-wife's child, a girl who isn't his own. He married a woman of loose morals, then was surprised when she left him. Oh, I've heard plenty around here, let me tell you. Is that the kind of bad judgment my grandchildren deserve? To be surrounded by people of poor choices? This is the example you're hoping to set for Michael's children?"

Gianna kept her voice quiet while a tempest rose within her. How dare Marie come here and start judging people? How dare she think her way was the best way? Being a grandmother didn't include the right to ridicule others. The Campbells were a wonderful family. "Seth is a marvelous man. And Tori is precious beyond words."

"It is time for you to go, Marie." Carmen stepped in from the kitchen area. She folded her arms and faced down Michael's mother with a degree of finality. "Gianna's choices are her own. She is strong. She is focused. She is healthy. I'm sure your son would be affronted at your treatment of the mother of his children. And that, Marie, is what you need to think about. Pray about. Because while grandparents have rights, those rights do not include belittling others. This is something, perhaps, you should take up with God."

Color heated Marie's cheeks. She stared at Carmen, hard and long, then raised her chin and turned toward Gianna, dismissing Carmen with silence. "I will see you at Easter."

"With no Realtor." Gianna made the point short and clear. "Our home is here."

Marie shrugged that off. "When you suddenly have two babies to watch, and a business to run, and Grandma takes ill, you'll come running for help."

Snappy comebacks raced through Gianna's mind, but she held her tongue. Marie liked to maintain a verbal upper hand. Gianna craved peace and grace. Reason enough to put five hours between herself and Marie, but she'd already done that, so rubbing salt in the wound was unnecessary. She turned toward Carmen as the door clicked shut. "You thought I was wrong about tutoring Tori."

Carmen shifted her attention from Marie's rigid, retreating back and considered Gianna. "I think you're letting fear guide you. Not faith. But I'm on your side, Gianna, no matter what decisions you make. This, of course, does not stop me from fervently praying for you to make the right choices."

"Those being the choices *you* think I should make." Gianna arched one brow as she faced her beloved grandmother.

"Indubitably." Carmen's pleased expression said Gianna was finally on track. "You fear loving Seth because of what he does, not who he is. And that fear isn't of God. It's of weakness."

"With good reason, I'd say."

Carmen didn't jump to agree this time. "Life hands most of us good reason to doubt and fear. But then it's up to us to decide what rules our lives. Doubt? Or God? Because worry is not of God." She faced Gianna straight on and continued, "You fear loving another policeman because of what we've lost, but I look at the past and know police work had little to do with what has happened to us. Any Good Samaritan might have stopped and helped that stranded couple on the thruway, but it happened to be your father, who happened to be a trooper. And it wasn't police work that got Michael killed, it was interrupting a robbery in progress. His police work didn't put him at risk, Gianna. Life did. And that's where God comes in." She moved toward the door and grabbed her lightweight jacket. "I'm running down to Tina's to grab a quiche for dinner. I ordered one this morning. Would you like a fancy coffee?"

She shouldn't, but the thought of creamy, caramel-laced coffee made her say yes. "But just a medium, Gram."

"Consider it done." The look Carmen aimed her way said she'd leave Gianna time to consider her words.

She'd disappointed Tori. And she'd most likely hurt Seth by backing away from her attraction to him, sending out conflicting signals like a fouled-up lighthouse inviting boats to run aground.

Her mother and Aunt Rose had gone back to Edgerton. They needed to reopen the homes they'd left in early winter. She'd promised to drive east to visit for Easter, but in the meantime, she had some serious thinking to do. Marie had placed her shots with her usual pinpoint accuracy, but Gianna wasn't the grief-stricken widow she'd been. She was strengthened by faith, hope and love. And good neighbors.

A small group of customers walked in just then. Gianna greeted them with a smile, and beyond the open door, she saw Seth, chatting with Reverend Smith and Titus. Seth bent to pet the dog, and the image he presented, the tall, resilient, rugged lawman, gentle enough to soothe a young dog and care for a child not his own…

Her heart tripped and fell right then.

Seth was the image of fatherhood she'd always loved, very like the earnest, funny, patriotic father she'd lost as a child. The easy grin, the quiet countenance, the strong and knowing silences.

A guardian. A protector.

Her heart longed for that very thing, but was that because she was falling in love with him? Or because she feared her old weaknesses and wanted someone else to take charge?

Love, she realized, watching him pet the tail-wagging

pup. Pure, sweet, unadulterated love. Joy coursed through her, paralleled with fear, an angst that needed to be resolved. She'd come this far with faith, hope and love. There was no reason she couldn't go further if she let herself. Now she had to just summon the courage to do just that.

CHAPTER SIXTEEN

S ETH SAW GIANNA'S NUMBER IN the call screen and answered the phone quickly that evening.

"I want to work with Tori. Tutor her. If you haven't found anyone else yet."

No way was Seth about to confess he hadn't called the other woman because he had been hoping Gianna would reconsider. He'd save that confession for later. Much later.

Tori would love this change of plans. Frankly, so would Seth. He didn't tiptoe around; he grabbed the offer like a drowning man grasps a lifeline. "Excellent. Monday, Wednesday and Friday good for you?"

"Yes. But if you're working any of the other afternoons, she can still come here."

Seth chalked up another plus in the "win" column and smiled, unseen.

"We'll get her work done and then she can sew. Or help in the store."

"She'll love that."

"Me, too."

His heart sighed at her words. He'd read the hesitation in her face and voice these past weeks. He knew she longed to draw closer, but fear kept her at bay.

He was a cop. He loved being a cop. And he'd dealt with a woman who tried to conform to an unsuited way of life before. The dismal failure of his marriage made him wiser and more cautious, but that caution fell by the wayside in Gianna's presence. "She'll be thrilled, Gianna."

"Us, too. I'm going back to Edgerton for Easter, though, so we can do the beginning of this week, then I'm gone from Holy Saturday through Easter Monday."

"When we start to enjoy the influx of tourism and summer folks."

"Yes."

"Good timing. Hey, go to your kitchen window."

"My kitchen window? Why—" She laughed and waved through the wide pane of glass when she spotted him grinning from across the street. "The yard is looking good."

"Flattening out innumerable vole trails in the grass was beneficial, right?"

"Don't tell me how you did it. I prefer to think of them like the little 'Woodsies' I played with as a kid, squeaking along in their hollow-tree homes. I'm sure you put them in some sort of witness relocation program for rodents. Right?"

"I'll keep my methods on the down low. Would you like to have supper together tonight?"

She stared from the window, and her hesitation gave him hope as he ticked the seconds off in his head. One... two...three...

"I can't, Seth."

He may have gotten a reluctant refusal, but he counted the interval as a victory. "Another time, then. Because you know I'll keep asking."

This uncertainty wasn't nearly as long and made his heart chug a little faster. "I hope you do."

"You can count on it. I'll tell Tori the news."

"Okay. Goodbye."

"Bye." He didn't just hang up the phone, though. He

waved across the street, to the window, knowing she could see him clearly.

And she waved back, smiling.

"Gianna?" Tori half whispered Gianna's name on Wednesday afternoon.

Carmen was busily chatting with the two customers in the store, so Gianna ducked into the kitchen. "What's up? Did you finish that internet United States map quiz this quickly? Awesome!"

"Yes, but it's not that." Worry darkened Tori's face as she pointed to the television in the living room. "Your grandma was checking the news earlier, but now this came on."

"This" was a special news bulletin about a police standoff in Clearwater, the small city at the southernmost boundary of Kirkwood Lake. Home to a state university and a dwindling population after a two-decade loss of manufacturing jobs, Clearwater had known its share of problems the past several years. The up-to-the-minute news coverage showed a campus lockdown at the SUNY school, small shopping centers with no discernible movement and a ring of various police fanning in multiple directions. The ticker running across the bottom of the screen said shots had been fired, causing multiple injuries. Reports of two policemen down were being investigated for accuracy.

"Dad's there. He patrols the area between the college and the south end of the lake. He's done that stretch for years."

Tori's fear tunneled Gianna back in time, to another little girl. A little girl who wouldn't kiss her daddy goodbye because he'd made her clean up her toys before he'd left for work. A little girl who'd never been able to kiss her daddy again.

"Tori, I—"

"Can we call him? Make sure he's all right?"

They couldn't, of course. "If we take his attention away from his job, we might put people in danger, Tori. Including him."

Tori's dark eyes searched hers. She met the child's fear with a strength and resolve she'd thought long gone. Tori's gaze darted from the television screen to Gianna and back again. "How will we know he's all right? What if he's hurt, Gianna?"

"We pray." Using the remote control, she switched off the coverage and grabbed Tori's hands. "Borrowing trouble is never in anyone's best interests. We'll pray for those hurt and for those trying to be peacemakers." *Blessed are the peacemakers, for they shall be called children of God.*

"Our Father, who art in heaven, hallowed be thy name…"

Tori's shaky voice joined hers. Gianna held tight to the girl's hands, hoping and praying peace would win the day.

"There is trouble?" Carmen came into the room and appraised their situation with a quick look.

"A police situation in Clearwater." Gianna let her lifted eyebrows explain the gravity of the situation.

"Then soup would be good," Carmen declared. "And brownies, they are quick and delicious when warm. You two can do the baking." Carmen crossed to the kitchen with typical quick, decisive movements. "I will cook. And then we can deliver them to the substation for when the men and women return."

"Dad loves peanut butter brownies."

"Well, who doesn't?" Carmen smiled at the girl and reached into a cupboard. She withdrew four boxes of brownie mix and nodded toward the table. "I'll use the counter for my work. The table is all yours. And if we get a customer, we will take turns in the store."

Busy hands.

Carmen Bianchi was a champion of busy hands, and her ploy worked. With an occasional break for customers, they had a big pot of chicken noodle soup and two half-sheet trays of peanut butter brownies ready in just over two hours. The sheriff substation was located outside the current restricted zone, and the empty parking lot when they pulled in said the deputies were still out in force.

A lieutenant greeted them as they came through the door. "Can I help you, ladies?"

"If you would carry the soup pot in, that would be good!" Carmen took him to the car while Gianna and Tori set up the trays of brownies on an empty side table in the back room. Once done, Tori placed the sign she'd made to welcome the deputies back to the station. "We love you guys! Thank you for keeping us safe!"

She'd used a rainbow array of markers, distinctly feminine, and signed her name at the bottom right. When the lieutenant lugged in the twelve-quart pot of soup, the chocolate-filled table drew his attention. He smiled. "They'll be grateful, ladies. I promise."

"Gianna?" Carmen moved closer, solicitous, covering the bases as usual, the perfect policeman's wife even this late in the game. "Are you all right?"

She was, Gianna realized. After years of hurting and avoiding anything to do with police work, the sights and smells of a substation seemed familiar and comfortable. Her father had toted her into their mountain barracks on his days off. And she'd often met Michael there when tight scheduling didn't allow him time to come home after a shift.

She thought she'd hate coming here, but the normalcy of the small and neatly appointed headquarters calmed her. "Fine, Gram. We'll head back home." She turned and nodded to the lieutenant. "We know you're busy."

His face said her words were an understatement, but

Tori's presence kept them from saying more. "Thank you so much."

"God bless you." Carmen shook his hand roundly before they left, and as they were driving back home, Tori's phone buzzed an incoming text: All well. Home late. Love you.

Gianna fought tears of relief as Tori recited the message out loud. Sneaking a glance toward Carmen, she saw a similar gleam in her grandmother's eye.

Seth had sounded an "all's well," letting them know he was okay.

Her heart sang with joy, and as Tori texted her father about the brownies, Gianna realized two things. First, she'd made it through a police crisis without falling apart.

And second, she never wanted Seth Campbell to have to face another without knowing he was beloved. Which meant she'd better come to terms with her past and pave a new road for her future.

"A winter storm warning? In April?"

Carmen directed Gianna's attention to the television set where the weather crew was taking particular delight in the anomaly of the late-winter storm barreling toward them on the cusp of an Alberta Clipper.

"But how can we get to Edgerton for Easter?"

Carmen sent her a look and Gianna slipped into the chair. "We can't."

"Not worth the risk, even if you weren't pregnant. They're talking nearly two feet of snow in some areas, poor visibility and drifts blocking east/west highways."

"Which says I-90 and I-86 are out of the question." Gianna stared at the set, then swung back to her grandmother. "Any chance of it missing New York?"

"There is not. Do you want to call them or shall I do it?"

Gianna reached for the phone, but an incoming call from her mother beat her to it. "There's a storm coming in," Sofia reported quickly. "I hate to miss you on Easter, but I don't want you and Mother traveling in a storm. Once things clear up, I'll come see you again, okay?"

Her mother sounded delightfully normal. And sweetly protective, looking out for her daughter and her two unborn grandchildren. "You don't mind, Mom?"

"Mind? Of course not. I'd be frantic thinking of you on the roads in the snow. That doesn't mean I won't miss you, but it's only one Easter Sunday out of so many. And next year we'll have the babies to dress. And I will buy a bonnet for my granddaughter—"

"Which she'll most likely pull off and toss to the floor," Gianna interjected.

"No matter, I will get one picture of her with it and be happy. You stay there, I will come and cook lamb for you next week. I love you, Gi-Gi."

Delight threaded its way up Gianna's spine. Her mother hadn't used that childhood nickname in years, a name her father had coined when she was a baby. "I love you, too, Mom."

She hung up the phone and stared at the western horizon. The distant band of gray seemed innocuous now, but if the meteorologists were correct, by tomorrow morning they'd be in the thick of a storm that would then bounce off the coast, spiral around and re-hit them on Easter Sunday as a nor'easter.

"A quiet Easter in the village," Carmen remarked. She pointed to the prettiness of yellow and white daffodils edging houses and shops dotting Lower Lake Road, Overlook Drive and Main Street. "By the time the snow melts, they'll be gone, so we better get our fill of looking now."

"Gianna?"

"Seth." Gianna moved to the kitchen door and wondered if he read the delight in her eyes. "What's up?"

"Snow." He pointed west. "Coming quick and heavy by morning. I know you were supposed to go back home tomorrow, and I'm on my way to work, but I wanted to make sure you saw the forecast."

"You were worried about me."

His shrug said he wouldn't pretend otherwise.

"I've canceled the trip home." When he looked relieved, she added, "Gram and I are going to have a quiet Easter right here."

"Actually, I was hoping you'd join Tori and me at my parents' for Easter dinner." He hooked a thumb toward the far side of the lake. "There will be a bunch of local Campbells there, but the storm is keeping some away. Having you and Carmen there would make the table seem fuller."

Kind. Sweet. Sensitive. And to-die-for good-looking. "Seth, we'd love to come."

Her warp-speed reply deepened his grin. "I don't have to convince you?"

"No."

"Beg?"

She laughed out loud. "Not in the slightest."

"Progress." He tipped his deputy's hat with the curve of his pointer finger and sent her an approving grin, a totally manly gesture that made her think of old movies and ride-the-range cowboys. "I like that, ma'am."

"Me, too."

"Well, now we know that Christmas will be quite beautiful here," Carmen chirped as they walked to the church for Easter services. Thick, wet snow clogged the old-style sidewalks. The plows had cleaned the roadways, but the walkways would stay impassable. And tomorrow's weather promised rain and mid-forties, so the return to winter would be short-lived.

"Dad, this is unbelievable." Tori gazed around the snow-filled town and made a face. "Have you ever seen this much snow on Easter?"

"Once. When I was little. We sledded down Cranberry Hill on Easter afternoon. After the egg hunt."

"Can we do that today?"

He laughed and slung an arm around Tori's shoulders. "If you'd like. The twins and Aiden will be at Grandma's house. They might get a kick out of sledding on Easter. Gianna?" He turned her way and hiked a brow. "What about up in Edgerton? Snow on Easter?"

"A dusting," she replied. She waved a hand to the snow-covered roofs, the heavy drifts slanting east to west. "Nothing like the lake effect you get here."

"It's not a deal-breaker?"

"For?" She met the question in his eyes straight on.

"Staying?"

Staying here, near Seth, forging new paths in this cozy, lakeside town. It would take a whole lot more than snow to send her packing. "Definitely staying. Right, Gram?"

Carmen waved a greeting to Tina and started up the snow-framed church steps. "Without a doubt."

As they stepped into the white clapboard church, a lone trumpet called the service to order, the sweet notes proclaiming Christ's empty tomb.

The tones rang simple and true, a note-by-note musical tribute. As voices joined in the second time around, Gianna felt the press of Seth's hand on her lower back. She turned.

He held out a book of hymns and leaned in. "We never have enough it seems, and it's even worse on holidays. Personally, I think it's the reverend's way of getting folks to talk together. Sing together. Pray together."

"Does it work?" Gianna whispered.

Seth held up the book in his hand and smiled when she reached out to grasp her side. "It appears so."

CHAPTER SEVENTEEN

DENSELY FORESTED HILLS SURROUNDING THE eastern shore pushed most of the Easter day snow to the far side of the lake. "A natural windbreak with a Nor'easter," Seth explained as he parked the car in his parents' shoveled driveway. "But Friday's snow came from the west and dumped on this shoreline big-time before going up-mountain, so it all evens out in the end."

"An equal-opportunity snowstorm." Carmen and Tori climbed out of the backseat as Gianna retrieved a cookie tray from the hatch of Seth's SUV. "You still thinking of sledding, Tori?"

"I can't wait," she exclaimed. The pure joy in her young face had come a long way from the woebegone child left in the cold at Seth's back door. "It's light out until almost seven-thirty, and that never happens in the winter."

"Good point." Seth pretended to be matter-of-fact, but Gianna sensed the growing satisfaction within him.

"I want to go sledding, too," Gianna added. "It would be great fun."

"Next year," Seth told her, sounding gentle and protective. He took Gianna's arm to keep her steady on the slick surface and added, "We'll make it a family outing." He grazed her rounded form with a meaningful look and reached ahead of them to pull open the storm door. "And while it wasn't necessary for you ladies to bring anything, I can't wait to dive into those cookies."

"Life's short. Eat dessert first." Gianna exchanged a knowing grin with Tori.

"Don't listen to her, Tori Elizabeth. Veggies are crucial to life."

Tori laughed as she propped the door open. "I like Gianna's way better, Dad."

"And why wouldn't you?" he muttered, teasing her. "I think you consider cookies and cake a foundation food group all by themselves. But if that's roast lamb I smell, I'm about the happiest guy alive right now."

"It's that easy?" Gianna teased as Carmen preceded her up the stairs. "An afternoon of good food puts you over the top?"

He bent and brought his mouth close to her ear. Really close. *Whisper close.* "The company I'm keeping puts me over the top," he answered softly, so no one else could hear. "The food's just a nice addition."

His face, so dear. The rumble of his voice, deep and distinct. His gaze on hers as he straightened, saying so much in the silence of an exchanged look.

"Gianna, let me help you with that." Seth's father reached out to take the cookie tray from her hands. "You might think I'm doing this to be nice while you lose the coat, but it's really to give me an advantage over my sons and grandchildren when they see this tray. Are those little cannolis I see?"

"They are."

"Well, you've won this man's heart." Charlie nipped a cannoli from the tray as he set it on the old oak server in the dining room and took a generous bite.

Gianna watched, waiting, not removing her jacket until the verdict was in.

Charlie's grin said she'd done good.

Jenny rolled her eyes, reached for Gianna's jacket and made maternal noises over the breadth of her belly as Seth helped her release one stubborn sleeve. Gianna looped her hands around her tummy and met Jenny's eye. "Huge, right?"

"Delightfully normal for two beautiful babies, I'd say. And you look wonderful, Gianna. Oh, Cass, can you hang Gianna's jacket on a hook? Or in the closet? Anyplace you find room, actually."

Cassidy. Gianna pivoted and came face-to-face with one of the most striking women she'd ever seen. Adding tall and willow-whip-thin to the descriptive mix made her long to see her feet again, but while Cassidy looked nothing like her siblings or parents, the smile she flashed Gianna was Campbell-friendly, through and through.

She disappeared with Gianna's and Seth's coats, then reappeared within seconds and extended her hand. "I'm Cass."

"Gianna, my sister Cassidy. Cassidy, my neighbors and tenants, Gianna Costanza and her grandmother, Carmen Bianchi."

"Nice to meet you." Cass took Gianna's hand and pulled her forward. "Come on out here. It's not quite as crazy as the kitchen at the moment, but give Mom fifteen minutes and it will all wind down to some degree of normalcy."

"I'd love to help." Carmen arched a brow to Seth's mother. "In Edgerton I was used to doing the big dinners, organizing, planning. It's different now, just the two of us, so if you wouldn't mind?" She swept the kitchen a hopeful glance.

"I'd love a hand out here." Jenny shooed the younger people toward the door. "Go. Talk. Relax. Carmen and I will load up the buffet in a few minutes."

"Not that I mind relaxing after this past week's never-ending shifts, but are you sure you don't need me,

Mom?" Cass lingered near the pass-through, waiting for her mother's reply.

"I'll grab you for cleanup," Jenny promised.

"Addie and I can double-team the dishes."

A shorter young woman stepped up into the living room from the enclosed front porch. "Hey, if Mom feeds us, I'll be glad to split cleanup with you. I'm so sick of anything that tastes like my own cooking that I came up early to beat the snow just so I could eat real food."

"Addie, this is—"

"Gianna." The petite Asian woman filled in the blank before Seth could say more. "I've heard all about you from Tori. Seth brought her down to Bonaventure a few weeks ago, and all she kept talking about was Gianna this and Gianna that. I'm the youngest Campbell."

"And the shortest." Seth rumpled his sister's hair and she made a face at him.

"You're such a kid, Seth. Hey, you better double-check your Lego castle on the porch. Somebody might have touched it since you were here last. The pieces could be out of order."

"You're funny, Addie. For a short chick."

"Uncle Seth lets us play with his Legos all the time!" Aiden streaked in just then, followed by the twins, and the burst of five-year-old energy hiked the noise level.

Addie hugged the kids, directed them toward Seth's pristine castle, then flashed him a grin. "I'll fix it later. Promise."

"If it keeps them occupied before the egg hunt, I'm okay with it."

"What a beautiful family." Carmen's voice drew attention to her vantage point in the dining room. She smiled at the two young women surrounded by blue-eyed, fair-haired Campbell men. "You are blessed to have each other. And so many!"

"My own personal United Nations," Jenny quipped as she carried a tray of twice-baked potatoes to the server. "Our families had been pretty much Celtic for way too long. It was time to mix things up a bit."

"No argument here." Cassie laughed and chucked Seth on the arm. "It was *almost* always nice to have big brothers stand up for you."

"And scare your dates away." Addie sent Luke and Seth scolding looks.

"Only the unworthy ones," Luke countered smoothly. "Which was ninety-nine percent of them, Addie."

"Don't remind me."

"I think we're ready." Jenny glanced back at the kitchen, nodded and motioned to the elongated table. "Cass, can you call your father in, please? And Luke and Rainey? Then we can join hands for grace."

They did, a large and varied gathering of people, one family, regardless of background or ethnicity.

I love this.

Peace pervaded the room, despite the jokes and laughter, and maybe because of it. A peace born of love and acceptance, an array of cultural blends and approval, a trickle-down warmth that came straight from Charlie and Jenny, Seth's parents.

Family, despite the obvious differences. Close-knit, even when far-flung.

Marie had often preached about family. *Famiglia*, the term she used for keeping others out. But the Campbells used the term to ask others in.

This was what Gianna wanted, what she'd longed for. Embracing acceptance, forbearance and humor, a family united in faith, hope and love. One look at the intensity of Seth's gaze said she could have her dream if she let courage conquer fear.

Could she?

The reverend's morning message made her see Christ's

courage in the cross. Could she grasp that courage and use it herself?

"While you're weighing the problems of the world, food's getting cold." Seth motioned to his brother Luke. "And with Luke's wedding two weeks away, I'm reminded that I need a date. Gianna Campbell, would you do me the honor of accompanying me to Luke and Rainey's wedding?"

Say yes. Drink from the cup. Believe.

"I'd love to."

"Good." He bent lower so that only she could hear his next words. "And you might want to think about being my date for any and all upcoming Campbell events." He made a face as if considering. "Town events, too. Like... forever."

Forever?

She raised her gaze to his and he shrugged as if they were talking about the weather or spring baseball. "Just something to think about."

"What if I don't need to think about it?"

This time it was his hand that paused and held up the line of hungry Campbells waiting to serve themselves.

"What if I think being by your side forever would make me and these babies the happiest people in the world?"

His jaw opened, then closed. A smile lit his face, a smile that went beyond joyful surprise. It was a grin that lit up the dark corners of her world. He put his plate down, reached out and kissed her soundly, in front of the entire Campbell clan, a kiss of promise and hope.

And she kissed him back.

With his plate growing cold and his arm firmly tucked around her shoulders, he turned toward the surrounding family. "I'm pretty sure Gianna just agreed to be my wife."

Gianna confirmed it with a quick nod. "He's correct."

"Which means..."

"A new family photo!"

"A wedding!"

"Babies!"

"Gianna, really?" Tori sneaked into her side amid the flurry of congratulations and questions. "You're really going to marry my dad? And be like my...stepmother?"

Gianna cradled Tori's sweet face between her two hands. "Yes. You and I will work together on schoolwork, sewing and the babies. With maybe some skiing and sledding on the side. Whaddya think?"

"I think yes!" Tori grasped her in a hug that said more than words ever could. "Gianna, this is the happiest day of my life!"

"Ditto." Seth grinned at Tori and palmed her head before shifting his attention back to Gianna. "I can't believe you caved."

"Blame the snow," she quipped back. "One look at how it piles up here made me realize I need someone with a strong back and a shovel. You fit the bill."

The light in his eyes said he saw behind the humor in her words. He read the leap of faith. The conviction. The chance she was willing to take to move forward.

And if the surrounding Campbell expressions were trustworthy, they'd been given a unanimous stamp of approval. And that felt beyond good...it felt simply marvelous.

EPILOGUE

"CENTER THE BABY TOWARD THE top of the blanket's diamond." Seth's intent look of concentration said he was putting his all into the swaddling lesson. "Then draw the left side of the diamond across."

"How precious is he?" Carmen whispered from the old oak rocker, where she held a tiny pink bundle against her chest.

"Adorable," Gianna whispered back.

"Then pull up the bottom and tuck it to the right and underneath. Kid, there is nothing in the instruction manual about how to do this if you're kicking, so could you please stop? Cut me some slack here."

Tori giggled out loud.

Jenny Campbell came into the living room of Seth's house and rolled her eyes. "It's going to be eighty-five degrees today. He doesn't need a blanket, Seth."

"Newborns and old people chill more easily. I read it last night."

The newborn kicked and squirmed, turned red in the face, then gave a lopsided look that almost passed for a smile. Seth stared down at him, bemused. "You had to wait until now to do that? Didn't I just change you?"

Jenny laughed as she folded laundry. "That's how it goes at this stage. I think he's getting even with you for the whole blanket thing. Leave him in his little outfit and lose the blanket."

"But I've been practicing." Seth made a funny face down at the baby boy and began the process of changing him all over again. "At this rate, I suppose I'll get plenty of practice."

"You can say that again." Gianna started to stand and three voices scolded her to sit and relax. She laughed but did as she was told. "I could get used to this. Tell me again how perfect they are."

"Absolutely, marvelously perfect. And as different as night and day."

"May I come in?"

Marie's voice interrupted the conversation. Five pairs of eyes turned toward the screened door. Gianna recovered first. "Marie, of course! Come and meet your grandchildren."

She came through the door, her motions timid, as if testing uncharted water. As she moved into the living room, her eyes swept the scene, lighting first on one baby, then the other.

She paused, midstep, uncertain, but then Seth lifted the baby boy and turned, depositing him into his surprised grandmother's arms. "Marie, meet Michael Joseph Campbell. Your grandson."

Her eyes rounded as she studied the newborn baby in her arms. Her mouth pressed tight, and her jaw quivered. And when little Mikey opened his eyes, looked up at her and clasped her finger, she sank into the nearest chair and wept.

Gianna crossed the room and sat down beside her, silent. Waiting. When Marie finally lifted her gaze, Gianna touched the baby boy's face with one hand. "He looks like his daddy. He looks like Michael."

"So much." Marie's voice caught on the words. "So very much."

"I knew it the minute they showed him to me. Those eyes. That strong chin. The big head."

Marie laughed and sighed. "Yes. And he is fine. They are both fine?"

"Perfect."

"And his name." She pressed a gentle kiss to the newborn's cheek and held him up, cheek to cheek, breathing in his scent. "You named him for Michael."

"And my father. It was the right thing to do. The best tribute I could offer."

"And my granddaughter?" Marie turned her attention across the room to Carmen. "What is her name?"

Carmen rose and brought the smaller twin over. She tucked her into Marie's other arm. "Isabella Sofia Bianchi Campbell. A ridiculous number of names for something so small."

"But lovely, yes?" Sofia and Rose came in from outside, a tray of coffees and sweets from Tina's Place in their hands. "Marie, you're here. Isn't this amazing? My Gianna, she has done this, brought these babies to us! I'll stop, I promise. I know I'm being loud—it's just when I think of all she's gone through, all the hours of sadness…and now this joy! This wonderful joy." Sofia set the coffees down and began hugging everyone in sight. "Two gifts from God. Heavenly Father's name be praised! I am beyond delighted, even though I have to drive across the state. Which is not a convenience."

Marie cleared her throat. She looked trapped, then awkward. With a deep breath she held tight to both babies but shifted her attention to Gianna. "I have come to see these babies, but also to apologize."

Gianna tried to wave her off, but Marie shook her head firmly.

"Let me finish." She dropped her eyes to the two quiet babies in her arms. Her face showed the wonder of life. Of birth. "I was becoming a bitter old woman. I pretended I had gone on with my life after losing my son, but in my heart I held such anger."

Gianna understood completely. She'd walked a similar path for far too long.

"When I realized you'd done this, that you'd decided to attempt a pregnancy, all that anger came surging up like a roll of thunder. I was so mad, so angry, that if you were successful, Michael would never see his son. Never hold his daughter. Never feed them, rock them. They would never see what a good, solid man he was because he wasn't here. You called me on it." She turned toward Carmen. "And I hated you right then, Carmen, because you hold life with such tender, loving care. I envied you. But now—"

The entire audience shifted forward, attentive.

"I went back to church. I talked to God. I told Him what a sinner I was, how angry I was, at Him, at you, at everyone. And He reminded me of something I did long ago, before my marriage fell apart, before Michael was in school, even." She motioned to the floral tote bag she'd carried in. Seth crossed the room, reached down and opened the tote. With Marie's nod of permission, he withdrew a simple hand-embroidered wall hanging. "As for me and my house, we will serve the Lord."

"From the book of Joshua," Carmen remarked. "Marie, that is beautiful work."

"When I was young, I took time for such things. Then I got angry and forgot to take that time. Now?" She smiled down at the two babies. "Now, so much is different."

"It is."

Marie drew a breath, then turned toward Gianna more fully. "I want to move here. To be close to these babies. And before you say no, let me again apologize for my anger. My mean-spiritedness. I believe I've conquered that, I believe I have what it takes to be a good, gentle nonnie. The kind of nonnie these babies would want me to be."

"To err is human. To forgive, divine."

Gianna didn't hesitate. She'd love to have the soft side of Marie Costanza in her corner. "I'd love that, Marie."

Marie's face relaxed. "Really?"

"Absolutely."

Seth moved closer and reached down for Isabella as she started to squirm. "I think it's an excellent idea. Babies should be surrounded by family. In fact, the middle-of-the-night shift is open for the taking."

Marie laughed.

Carmen jutted her chin toward the lakefront. "Why don't you stay in the apartment with me while you look for a house?"

Gianna almost choked.

Sofia raised her brows but said nothing, a good choice for all concerned.

Marie went straight to the point. "You don't think we'd kill each other?"

Carmen laughed out loud. "Not now," she told Marie. "I like seeing the Marie I knew for so long back home. And if you'd like to keep busy, we could use someone helping people in the shop. Gianna will be working to care for the babies, and Tori has finished school, but I can't steal her all the time. Seth and Gianna will need her help over here, too."

"I've never held a job." Marie offered the words like a confession.

"Then no time like the present to learn." Carmen reached out and put a hand on Marie's arm. "You can consider it an act of service if that's easier. You'll meet people. And you'll still have plenty of time to house shop."

Marie's gaze swept the room. Disbelief made her hesitate, but then she admitted, "I wasn't sure what kind of reception I'd receive today. You've humbled me, and we all know that's a big step forward."

"We're family, Marie." Gianna reached out and hugged her former mother-in-law. "All of us here. *Famiglia*. And that's what families do."

Marie's eyes filled again, but these were joyful tears. She turned toward Carmen and offered a firm nod. "Then I will take you up on your generous offer. I'd love to stay with you, Carmen Bianchi. Do you still play a mean game of Scrabble?"

Carmen grinned. "I do. But I don't want to make you mad all over again."

Marie lifted little Michael and kissed his soft, rounded cheek. "I don't believe anger is even possible anymore. And why would I get angry about beating you?"

Carmen laughed.

Seth slipped an arm around Gianna's shoulders and helped her up. "You need to rest. We have plenty of help here—"

"Maybe too much," Sofia offered. She winked at Rose, but it was Carmen who took the hint and moved toward the door. "I'm going to take Marie across the road to get settled. If you two take the daytime shift, maybe Marie and I can help overnight?"

Seth's look of relief said he'd be grateful. "I go back to work tomorrow, so a few hours of straight sleep would be appreciated. And knowing the babies are in such good hands?" He smiled at both women. "Better yet."

Marie handed little Michael to Jenny. She turned to accompany Carmen, but before she left she stopped in front of Seth. She reached up and laid her hand against his cheek. "Despite what I have lost, I have gained so much." She patted his cheek and smiled. "Welcome to the family, Seth Campbell."

Seth pulled her into his arms for a big old-fashioned

Campbell hug. Gianna watched, her eyes smarting with emotion.

"It's nice to be here, Marie."

It was more than nice, thought Gianna as she and Seth moved up the stairs to their room. A new business, a husband, a stepdaughter who had won her heart instantly, a new home, two babies...

And the combination of multiple families that made it all possible. The sacrifice and love of so many mothers, trying to go the distance for their children.

"I love you, Seth."

He smiled down at her, tucked in the covers and grazed her cheek with his hand. "I know. Me, too. Thanks for rushing into marriage with me. It gave me extended baby-bragging rights at work."

She laughed and sighed because the softness of the pillow felt so good. "I do what I can, deputy."

His soft kiss said he appreciated that and more. So much more. She fell asleep, knowing she'd found more than a new start in Kirkwood. She'd found a new life.

DEAR READER,
Science is a marvel. We live in an age where so much can be done to cure disease, aid the chronically ill and help infertile couples. Because of that, we question the wisdom of what we do daily. Knowing we *can* do something, doesn't always mean we *should*.

Gianna Costanza and her husband, Michael, wanted a family. They seized the scientific means available to them and then life changed. Suddenly. Drastically. But when Gianna's conscience began to dwell on her two frozen embryos, her faith brought her to the only decision she could make. She longed to offer them a chance at life. Their only chance. She made a bold move, and did it at great personal sacrifice, because that's what parents do.

Seth Campbell's disastrous marriage showed him the error of his ways. He learned that both people need to be invested in faith and family for a marriage to work. He lost his wife and the daughter of his heart. Experience has taught him so much, but too late. Or is it? Not with God. With God, timing is in his hands, his care. And when prayer and faith bring his precious child back to him, Seth begins to realize that even though he's a big, strong sheriff's deputy, God's looking out for *him* while he looks out for others.

Sacrificial love. It's what Christ exampled to us. It's what we saw in the story of Ruth in the Old Testament. It's what the true mother demonstrated when Solomon offered to have the child cut in two. The true mother was willing to sacrifice her time with her son to save his life.

I hope you loved reading this sweet story! I delight in hearing from readers. You can reach me at loganherne@ gmail.com, visit my website at ruthloganherne.com or hang out with me on Facebook. As always, I look forward to hearing from you, and thank you for reading Seth and Gianna's love story!

Ruthy

KIRKWOOD LAKE
RECIPE CORNER

Grandma's Spiced Vanilla Bread Pudding

This is a big favorite in Kirkwood Lake
and here at Blodgett Family Farm!

Preheat oven to 325 degrees.
Lightly spray 11" x 7" pan with cooking spray

Whisk or beat together thoroughly:
6 eggs, beaten (whisked or eggbeater or mixer)
1 cup sugar
2 teaspoons cinnamon
1 teaspoon nutmeg
2 teaspoons vanilla

When fully mixed, beat or whisk in:
1 ¾ cups milk
Break up dried or somewhat dry bread. Italian bread,
regular bread, French bread, cinnamon bread… or pieces
of bagel… all work well to soak up the custard above.

Add enough bread (usually about 6 to 10 slices,
depending on kind of bread) to give the pudding a
"stuffed with bread" appearance. I like my bread pudding
a little on the dry side.

It should look similar to this:

Pour into the prepared pan and then settle that pan into a larger baking pan with about 1" of water in the bottom, creating a steaming effect. Bake at 325 degrees until golden and top of pudding looks dry-ish.... Eat warm or cold with whipped cream, vanilla ice cream or all on its own.

A wonderful cool weather treat but we like to make it all year on the farm because everyone that helps here loves it!

ALSO BY RUTH LOGAN HERNE

If you loved this story by Ruthy, here's a list of other
Ruth Logan Herne books you'd probably enjoy!

Ruthy's Amazon Author page and books:
http://amzn.to/1v26FHw
★ ★ ★
INDEPENDENTLY PUBLISHED BOOKS:
Running on Empty
Try, Try Again
Safely Home
Refuge of the Heart
More Than a Promise
The First Gift
From This Day Forward
Christmas on the Frontier
The Sewing Sisters' Society
A Most Inconvenient Love
★ ★ ★
NORTH COUNTRY SERIES
Waiting Out the Storm
Season of Hope
Winter's End
★ ★ ★
SOUTHERN TIER ROMANCE
Reunited Hearts
Small Town Hearts
A Family to Cherish
The Lawman's Second Chance
★ ★ ★

FROM WATERFALL PRESS/AMAZON/
INDEPENDENT
Welcome to Wishing Bridge
At Home in Wishing Bridge
Finding Peace in Wishing Bridge
Embracing Light in Wishing Bridge
Reclaiming Hope in Wishing Bridge
Kindling Christmas in Wishing Bridge
★ ★ ★

FROM WATERBROOK PRESS/PENGUIN/
RANDOM HOUSE
Back in the Saddle
Home on the Range
Peace in the Valley
★ ★ ★

LOVE INSPIRED BOOKS
Mended Hearts
Yuletide Hearts
His Mistletoe Family
★ ★ ★

KIRKWOOD LAKE SERIES
Falling for the Lawman
The Lawman's Holiday Wish
Loving the Lawman
Her Holiday Family
Healing the Lawman's Heart
★ ★ ★

GRACE HAVEN SERIES
An Unexpected Groom
Her Unexpected Family
Their Surprise Daddy
The Lawman's Yuletide Baby
Her Secret Daughter
★ ★ ★

SHEPHERD'S CROSSING SERIES
Her Cowboy Reunion

A Cowboy Christmas (with Linda Goodnight)
A Cowboy in Shepherd's Crossing
Healing the Cowboy's Heart
★ ★ ★
GOLDEN GROVE SERIES
A Hopeful Harvest
Learning to Trust
Finding Her Christmas Family
★ ★ ★
KENDRICK CREEK SERIES
Rebuilding Her Life
The Path Not Taken
A Foster Mother's Promise
★ ★ ★
FROM BIG SKY CONTINUITY/LOVE INSPIRED
BOOKS:
His Montana Sweetheart
★ ★ ★
FROM SUMMERSIDE PRESS:
Love Finds You in the City at Christmas
★ ★ ★
From Barbour Publishing:
Homestead Brides Collection
★ ★ ★
FROM ZONDERVAN/HARPER COLLINS
All Dressed Up in Love
★ ★ ★
CONTRIBUTING AUTHOR
"MYSTERIES OF MARTHA'S VINEYARD"
Available at Guideposts.com

A Light in the Darkness
Swept Away
Catch of the Day
Just over the Horizon
★ ★ ★

CONTRIBUTING AUTHOR
"SAVANNAH SECRETS" MYSTERY SERIES
Available at Guideposts.com

A Fallen Petal
Patterns of Deception
Jingle Bell Heist
★ ★ ★
CONTRIBUTING AUTHOR
"MIRACLES AND MYSTERIES OF MERCY
HOSPITAL" SERIES:
Prescription for Mystery
Merciful Secrecy
★ ★ ★
FROM GUIDEPOSTS' "LOVE'S A MYSTERY"
SERIES:
Love's a Mystery in Sleepy Hollow, NY
Love's a Mystery in Cut and Shoot, Texas
★ ★ ★
FROM GUIDEPOSTS' "WHISTLE STOP CAFÉ
MYSTERIES" SERIES:
As Time Goes By
That's My Baby

ABOUT THE AUTHOR

MULTIPUBLISHED, BESTSELLING AUTHOR RUTH LOGAN Herne is having the time of her life writing novels, running a rapidly growing and absolutely amazing pumpkin farm (a retirement project that has grown in exponential and rather fun fashion!). Author of over seventy novels and novellas, published by multiple houses, Ruthy is the mother of six with a seventh daughter of her heart, amazing grandkids and Godchildren, and toss in a few dogs and cats for good measure. Married to her high school sweetheart "Farmer Dave", Ruthy loves God, her family, her country, dogs, mini-donkeys, chocolate and coffee... Chocolate and coffee might be higher up the list on given days. She loves to hear from people... email her at loganherne@ gmail.com or friend her on Facebook at Ruth Logan Herne or her Blodgett Family Farm page! She'd love to hear from you!